The Diamond Cutter

by

Van Blakely

BANTRY BAY PUBLISHING
CHICAGO · LOS ANGELES

ISBN: 9781724167484

Published by Bantry Bay Publishing, Chicago • Los Angeles
www.bantrybaybooks.com
To contact the author or publisher, email
bantrybaypublishing@gmail.com, or call (312) 912-8639

Cover photo by Dmitrii Stoliarevich

Dedicated to the music of Tom Scholz.

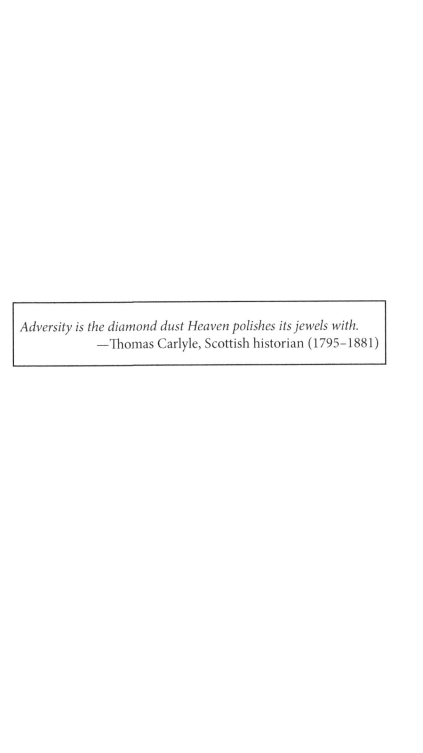

Adversity is the diamond dust Heaven polishes its jewels with.
—Thomas Carlyle, Scottish historian (1795–1881)

A Letter from the Author

To my beautiful daughters on your respective 16th birthdays:

Writing this story is out of character for your father. I don't profess to be a writer or creative thinker. However, something inside me possessed me to attempt, in my own way, to describe the indescribable. I eventually figured out what was driving this passionate effort.

As you meander your way through this yarn, you will quickly identify the main participants' youthful, immature flaws while also recognizing the genesis of their character and integrity. Remember to search out supportive and compassionate champions who know how to dream and share your dreams, who live in the present moment, whose hearts are focused on their eulogies rather than their possessions and résumés, and who will help you heal a ruptured spirit and settle a restless mind.

True happiness is generated and transformed when a human being's evolving and maturing inner peace travels through the soul's prism, allowing one to witness the world through the optical lens of another and genuinely and consistently place another's soul before one's own. It's about empathy and then charity. If you choose to give the gospels a chance, their respective and consistent message plainly encourages us all to follow a similar path: to simply and honestly love and forgive one another while taking care of the downtrodden, gifts bestowed upon each of us by grace. Lastly, this world is full of energy, magic, and mystery few humans fully comprehend. Be watchful of those qualities.

The moment someone you truly love passes away, the heart immediately longs to somehow describe the aforementioned indescribable. That nebulous, heartfelt feeling before heading into the abyss of despair momentarily searches for a place to scream out to the world what a beautiful soul the world has just lost.

On a crisp October evening in 1998, your Grandma Jean unexpectedly left this world without having the chance to meet you. When you someday ponder the main characters' wonderful attributes of friendship, compassion, selflessness, empathy, strength, and spiritual maturity, you will know your grandmother's heart and the love she would have had for each of you.

I love you.

Dad

About the Music

The song "Long Time" by Tom Scholz was the genesis, the catalyst, and the cornerstone of the The Diamond Cutter. Links to various classic rock songs of the era are intertwined throughout the story, each song carefully selected to capture the unique rhythm and tone of various scenes and situations while accentuating the spirit, mood, and message of the story. The music also acted as bookmarks used to identify and harvest periodic waves of creativity during the story's development. The story could never have been written without the music. The ultimate magic and miracle of the story comes from the music itself. When sidetracked while writing the story, I often found myself reverting to Scholz's epic song. Music creates, preserves, and awakens memories. The soundtrack from the second generation of the rock and roll era, commonly known as the "cassette era," was further utilized to highlight that time period.

An index of the music can be found on Page 134.

If you'd like to listen to the author's musical inspirations as you read, a playlist has been created on Spotify. The link:

https://spoti.fi/2pKtzsB

If you've never had the joy of experiencing Big Sky Country, visit the link shown below. It will help you visualize the sites and scenery that play major characters in this story, and will help you understand the role music had in the writing of the story.

https://wi.st/1QK4VfH

"Music... will help dissolve your perplexities and purify your character and sensibilities, and in time of care and sorrow, will keep a fountain of joy alive in you."
— Dietrich Bonhoeffer (German theologian – 1906-1945)

Chapter 1

A computer tablet rests on the lap of a man clad in gray pinstripes and carefully matched wing-tipped shoes. As he flips through screens of commodity and financial data, a British siren sounds in the distance. The London rain pelts the top of the black limousine as it makes its way through the city. The vehicle pulls over to the curb, and the driver jumps out with a black umbrella. The driver navigates his way around the humming engine and arrives with cover as he opens the door for his client. The businessman, who has a noticeable limp, chooses to put his arm around the driver so the umbrella can shield them both as they make their way to the doors of the massive British Museum.

As they approach the entrance, a doorman quickly opens the door. Once the businessman is inside, a curator offers to take his full-length raincoat and introduces himself and several other museum administrators. After polite introductions and brief conversations, the anonymous businessman reaches into his lapel and pulls out an envelope. An administrator graciously accepts the generous donation, asking the businessman to walk with him. The group walks silently through the museum until they reach an environmentally controlled room with state-of-the-art retina security. The curator directs the businessman to a table where an ancient document lies. As the businessman approaches, he pauses slightly, showing his respect for the inanimate but powerful book. He lowers himself with care into the wooden library chair, taking a deep breath as he ponders his next move.

***

It's a crisp fall Friday night in western Montana. The black sky is vast and dense with stars. The lights of the small city echo the stars above, constellations of light surrounded by unbroken darkness. On the horizon, a speck of light begins to move, growing brighter. As it moves closer, a faint pumping sound cuts the air, and a helicopter materializes. The lights of the aircraft's undercarriage suddenly focus on the elevated landing pad of an eight-story hospital. The mechanical dragonfly touches down.

Peering through the windowed doorway, medical staffers wait for the pilot's signal. Seconds stretch on, and then it's a go: The staff spills out, and the roof erupts in organized chaos. EMTs lift two stretchers from the rear of the Life Flight unit, carrying a man and woman, victims of a highway crash. Inside the ER, there is already bedlam.

In the triage area, a Montana Highway Patrol officer sits with a young drunk, who is handcuffed and sporting a few cuts and bruises. A nurse begrudgingly hands him an ice pack and a towel. More EMTs rush in through the ambulance doors, wheeling the couple's young son, who has only just arrived.

In one of the treatment rooms, two nurses and a physician's assistant bark instructions back and forth over the unconscious mother. A third nurse comes in, his arms full of fresh supplies.

"I can't get her stabilized," the male nurse says. "Where's the goddamn doctor?"

"Dr. Wells is on the way. They just prepped and stabilized the father for surgery."

Suddenly, the mother flatlines. The nurses yell for help, grabbing ventilation equipment and defibrillator paddles. Finally, the doctor arrives and immediately begins methodically taking charge of the scene. Dr. Marianne Wells is highly confident, intelligent, and a leader, a seasoned ER doctor clearly at her best under these intense circumstances. She is petite in stature, with an earthy, subtle beauty—straight black hair pulled back and warm dark eyes. Under her direction, the medical team works quickly and efficiently; they sense a particular urgency behind Dr. Wells's calm. The young mother's heart restarts after the first electric current passes through her body, and she attempts to sit up as she gasps for air. Dr. Wells quickly diagnoses a collapsed lung and implements assisting ventilation.

Finally, after what seems like an eternity, the young mother is stabilized, and the medical staff breathes a little easier. The male nurse reminds Dr. Wells about the young couple's son in Exam Room Two. Marianne pauses momentarily to collect herself before saying, "Of course. I'll be there in a minute."

The young boy sits in shock with a male nurse by his side;

he doesn't look up when Marianne enters. She smiles and squats down to his level so she can look him in the eyes. "I'm Dr. Wells," she says. "And you must be Brian." She cradles his hand for a moment before taking his chart from the nurse. He's in stable physical condition, and she sets the chart to the side. "You know, my best friend's husband's name is Brian. I love that name. How are you, sweetheart?"

The boy shudders with fright and winces at the soreness caused by the accident.

"Brian, do you remember what happened?"

"Where are Mom and Dad? Some people pulled me out of the car—I was sleeping." The boy wipes his face with the sleeve of his hooded sweatshirt. "Mom and Dad wouldn't talk to me. They were bleeding."

"You were in a car accident, honey, and your parents got hurt. Some great doctors are taking care of them right now." She puts her hands on his face. "We're going to take very good care of your mom and dad." She stands and hugs him, looking over his head at the pediatric nurse, who nods back at her, her respect for Marianne evident.

Marianne walks down the hall to her doctor's quarters. She shuts the door behind her and puts her files on the table. She closes her eyes and breathes deeply. This one hits close to home.

Van Blakely

Chapter 2

Fall 1978

A purple letterman's jacket that displays a yellow *P* and the embroidered name Marianne hangs on the bedpost. The alarm clock goes off, waking the teenage girl. It is 5:30 a.m. Marianne begrudgingly turns the clock off, stretches, and wipes her eyes. She puts on a t-shirt and sweatpants and opens her bedroom door. Thinking she's the only one up, she tries not to wake her host family and walks silently down the hallway of the upscale home, enters the bathroom, brushes her teeth, and then quickly yanks a brush through her thick, black hair before placing it in a ponytail. She is naturally beautiful behind the tomboy facade. She puts on her running shoes, quickly throws her homework and workout gear into her backpack, and heads for the kitchen.

As Marianne enters the kitchen, she is startled by the resident father, who is standing at the kitchen island, sipping a cup of coffee and reading the morning newspaper. He greets her with a warm smile, followed by a paternal hug. He looks at his watch, reminds her she's a little late for practice, and offers her a ride on his way to work. She declines, grabs an orange for her backpack, and pulls on her hooded sweatshirt. She bolts out the back door. The father observes with approval, briefly pausing to recall her plight before returning to his morning cup and reading. Marianne starts her jog to school.

(*Shadows of the Night by Pat Benatar*)

It's a brilliant fall morning in Missoula—the leaves are gold, and the sky is sharp blue. Seventeen-year-old Marianne Sherman jogs down the Rattlesnake Creek trail among the changing maples. As she runs over the bridge spanning the Clark Fork River, the steam of her breath hangs in the air. Her jog ends at Hellgate High School's front steps, which she takes quickly. She drops her backpack in the locker room, says hello to a couple teammates, and turns the wheel on her locker. As she changes into her basketball shoes, she reflects on a simpler time.

***

In the late 1960s, the Sherman family resided on Flathead Lake, the largest natural freshwater lake west of the Great Lakes, 70 miles north of Missoula, Montana. Marianne had lived her whole life on the southern shore of the lake in the town of Polson, located on the Flathead Indian Reservation, which is where the Bitterroot Salish, Kootenai, and Pend d'Oreilles tribes were forced to live in the late 1800s. Her dad, who was half Salish, was a high school math teacher and football coach. Her mom was a California blonde who'd moved to Montana for college and stayed for Mr. Sherman. She was a full-time nurse at St. Joseph's.

The Sherman house, located next to a cherry orchard, was small and a little crowded, but to Marianne, it was a little Eden. She spent her childhood in and out of the woods and the lake, wrestling with her dad and her sister, Jennifer, and cooking with her mother. Her grandmother Esther lived nearby in a cottage along a stream at the foot of the Mission Mountains. She was a Salish medicine woman, and her home was a place of amazing smells, good stories, and warm blankets. Marianne and Jennifer loved spending weekends there, chopping firewood and making jam. In the summers, the Andersons arrived at the lake, and Marianne and Amanda Anderson spent every second together, with Jennifer tagging along.

***

Dr. Wells's pager goes off, calling her back to a patient who had come in before the accident victims—an ALS patient who had decided suicide was the answer to his desperate situation. Even though he was unsuccessful, it remains a difficult situation. Marianne reenters the waiting room to speak with the patient's family about the ethical and legal issues surrounding the man's living will that she must follow, including a do-not-resuscitate order. The wife of the patient looks drained, not only from the night's trauma, but from the years spent dealing with her husband's disease. After discussing the alternatives, the two women enter the patient's exam room.

The final stages of ALS are terrible to contemplate, let alone experience. The disease makes it difficult, and then impossible, to accomplish everyday tasks, such as buttoning a shirt or tying shoes. It eats away at a person's ability to use their own muscles to walk, use their hands, or even talk and eventually swallow; all while the brain is functioning normally. Knowing what's coming, its sufferers are instilled with a fear of where they'll be physically in a month, in six months, or in a year. There are no effective treatments for ALS, and there are no survivors.

Dr. Wells sits quietly with the patient and his grief-stricken wife. Suddenly, the patient gasps for air as nurses attempt to comfort him. After an agonizing few minutes, he passes away. The nurses and doctors call the death and begin to organize their thoughts and tasks. After her colleagues depart, Marianne sits next to the patient. She bows her head, collecting her thoughts and pausing for a brief, silent prayer. She looks out the hospital window where the sky has begun to brighten. It's been a difficult night.

She heads out to the hallway and is immediately called into another room. A patient thrashes on his bed while two nurses attempt to restrain him. Marianne wades into the situation, briefly gaining control before an arm slams her across the chest, knocking her back on her heels. She's immediately back in the fray, yelling for additional help. Having sedated the disoriented patient, she looks down at her scrubs. She's covered in something vile. The patient had lost control of his bowels.

Another long shift in the ER over, Dr. Wells heads to the parking lot. The morning sun begins to peek over Mount Sentinel as she stops at a kiosk for a coffee. Driving across town, she passes Hellgate High School. She manages a pondering smile.

***

After practice, young Marianne rushes from the girls' locker room to her first-period physics class, pulling her wet hair up into a ponytail on her way down the hall. She's wearing Levi's 501s and a faded sweatshirt under her weathered purple letterman's jacket. A couple of guys check her out as she goes by, but she ignores them and keeps moving.

She arrives at her physics class a little early and scans her homework, absentmindedly fiddling with the locket around her neck, an antique gift she wears every day. Her classmates trickle into the classroom and settle in at other tables. Two geeky boys join Marianne at her table; she glances up to say hi and returns to her notebook. As the teacher walks up to the front of the classroom and the bell sounds, there's a ruckus at the doorway. Two football players in scarlet-and-gold game jerseys are taking up space, laughing and chatting with their carbon-copy girlfriends. Behind them, Amanda Anderson is making a show of being blocked, tapping her foot and waving. She's Marianne's childhood best friend and a kind of adoptive sister. She's decked out in a cheerleading uniform, her blonde hair blown back from her face and her pink lip gloss carefully in place. "Hello? Billy? Mike? Other people are trying to get in here. Surely your erections can wait." She pushes past them and plops down next to Marianne.

"Hey, Amanda." Marianne smiles. "Having a good morning?"

"Oh my God, they're disgusting. I swear all that rerouted blood flow seriously reduces their brain capacity. Run interference, will you? My panties are riding up my ass crack."

Marianne laughs and blocks the view as Amanda fixes the situation.

"You're the greatest. Present," Amanda calls as the teacher begins roll call. "So, I missed you at breakfast. I was gonna get up early and make pancakes and everything." She digs in her bag, shuffling through papers and notebooks, until she finds her compact mirror. "Not that that happened. I don't know how you do it." Amanda appraises the status of her face and snaps the compact shut. "You have morning practice?"

"Yeah, I ran to school. Your dad didn't say? Oh, shhh."

The girls fall quiet as the teacher finishes attendance and launches into the daily drone.

Amanda nudges Marianne out of a daydream as the physics teacher passes out a quiz. "Thank God this is a work group quiz," Amanda says.

Marianne rolls her eyes. Amanda's smart, but she doesn't care about physics, and this is how it always goes. Marianne grabs the quiz and quickly works through it. Amanda finishes up her history homework and keeps an eye on the two geeky boys in the group, who're pretending to help, but mostly are just gawking at Marianne.

In the rush after the bell rings, Amanda places an envelope in front of Marianne. She stands and kisses the top of Marianne's head. "See you at the pep rally," she says, shaking imaginary pom-poms on her way out the door. Marianne knows what's in the envelope before she opens it: a card encouraging her on the anniversary of her family's deaths. For all her chatter and bluster, Amanda always remembers.

***

On a cool September night, they were driving back from Grandma Esther's, her dad at the wheel and her mom's voice a smooth, lulling current. Jennifer, next to Marianne in the backseat, was completely out, her feet curled up under her, and Marianne kept nodding off, too. Huckleberry, the family dog, rested between them, his head on Marianne's knee. She was awakened by a terrible sound—a screeching, followed by the crunch of glass and metal— and then the smell of burning rubber was everywhere. The cold air rushed in where the passenger windows should have been, and the doors came in at her at funny angles. Jennifer was screaming, and so was the dog, their voices coming together in one long, continuous howl. Everything was quiet around that scream. Marianne said, "Shhh, Jenny," but Jennifer kept going. "Mama," Marianne said to the front seat, "Jennifer won't stop."

Her mother didn't say anything. She tilted forward and over to the side toward Marianne's father, her profile still, her skin a weird blue-gray in the moonlight. Marianne didn't understand why she wouldn't tell Jennifer to be quiet. "Dad," she said, "make her stop. She's getting Huck riled up." She could see his shoulder and his dark head over the seat back in front of her. She squirmed to catch his eye, but when she did, a pain shot through her leg, a kind of pain that stopped everything. When she woke up again, blue and red lights flickered over her mother's frozen profile. Her sister was gone. Marianne watched her disappearing through a now-open car door, being wheeled away on a cart, tucked under blankets, her hair a dark smudge against the white linens. Marianne wanted a blanket, too. Somewhere, Huck was still whimpering. Grown-ups in uniform were pulling her from her seat, asking her questions, and strapping her to her own little cart. "I can stand," she said, but she couldn't.

"What's your name?" said a man in a familiar outfit. Marianne focused—it was Wilson from the hospital, from the Sunday softball team with her dad.

"You know my name," Marianne said. His wife was a nurse, just like her mom.

"I need you to answer these questions, Mare-bear," he said. "Help me out. It's a kind of test." He smoothed her hair and started to push the cart. "What year is it? What street do you live on?"

When the cart turned, the car came into view. Everything looked strange under the pulsing lights. She saw the way the car crumpled in on one side and saw the nose of a red pickup pushing into the space it had made for itself. Her father sat upright in his seat, his skin matching her mother's waxy blue. He stared straight ahead, right at her, through the spiderwebbed windshield. He looked surprised.

Wilson and someone else bent by her cot, fiddling. Marianne strained to see around them and caught sight of a tribal police officer and a paramedic standing near some bystanders at the side of the road. The paramedic crouched down next to something on the ground and then shook his head and stood. She saw that it was Huck. The little crowd moved off, and the officer drew his gun. The whimpering stopped.

Back by the car, a tribal police officer stood next to a man she didn't know. The man was yelling and waving his arms in the air. "You've got this shit wrong, Chief," he kept saying. There was a little blood on his forehead. "Bunch of dirty fucking Indians."

The officer grabbed the man's arms, pinning them behind him. She saw now that it was Officer Adler, her dad's best friend, in the uniform. She strained at the straps of her cot, trying to get his attention. She was being lifted; she heard sounds of sliding metal. The stranger was in cuffs now, and Officer Adler was marching forward toward the wreck of her family's car. When they reached the driver's side, Officer Adler pushed the man forward, planting his face against the cracked glass above her father's open eyes. Then Wilson blocked Marianne's view, doors slammed shut, and they were in motion. Somewhere, a siren wailed. When she woke in the hospital, Esther was by her bedside, and Jennifer was already dead.

Chapter 3

The Missoula Hellgate High School pep assembly is under way. Students pile into the gymnasium as the band pumps out a snappy tune. It's a rowdy, excited crowd. The perennially underachieving Hellgate football team has somehow started the season with a 3-0 record for the first time in 15 years, and now Hellgate is scheduled to play the Butte Bulldogs at home. It's been 20 years since Hellgate last defeated Butte, and the legend of the tough kids from the historic Mining City looms large.

The gym is awash in the scarlet, gold, and black of football players in their game jerseys and cheerleaders in uniform. The student body president comes up onto the podium and speaks into the microphone, getting the room riled up. He calls Coach Halloran up to join him, and the crowd goes nuts. In the sea of red and gold, there's a quiet spot: Brian Callaghan, quarterback of the football team, son of a prominent Missoula attorney, and Amanda's long-term boyfriend. He is smart, quietly confident, balanced, and perceptive beyond his years—a good all-around kid. He's standing with his buddy Steve Myers, a tight end on the team and one of his steadfast followers.

Brian watches his coach struggle up the podium with his bad knees and beer belly. As Coach Halloran steps up to the microphone, Brian rolls his eyes at Steve and says, "Buckle your bullshit waders."

Steve fakes a laugh. He's pretty into the whole thing, but he doesn't want to look bad in front of Brian.

Coach Halloran clears his throat and launches into his speech. He boasts of his team's success, dedication, and perseverance despite the fact that no one in the state gave them a chance and then starts in on what they are up against. At the words "Butte Bulldogs," a ripple passes through the room. "I hear you," Coach Halloran says. "I hear you. And I agree we've got our work cut out for us. But you think this team's afraid of a little hard work?" When the roar quiets, he continues. "And I gotta tell you, in the 17 years I've been coaching here at Hellgate, I haven't seen a team like the one we've got here. This team here, this unique set of men—I'm gonna be honest with you. I sincerely feel that this is the team that's gonna kick those Bulldogs back to Butte." Coach Halloran pauses, seeming to deliberate. "And you know what? I'm gonna tell you something else. That silver bullet they've got? The great Seamus McElroy? Word is he was hurt in the closing minutes of last week's game with Great Falls CMR. Word is he hasn't been in practice the entire week." In the crowd, something shifts. This is the most excited the players have been all year; they're restless with anticipation. "Now, I'm not saying we wouldn't still whoop them if he were on the field. But what I am saying is that is some sweet news."

Steve turns to Brian. "Well, that first part may have been bullshit," he says, "but without McElroy? This is it. This is our year."

"Yeah, sure," Brian says. Around them, the rally is drawing to a close.

"What's wrong with you today?"

"Listen, we've been playing against McElroy and those Butte kids since Pop Warner, since Little League. I've never come close to beating them at anything—basketball, baseball, football. Nothing. I just don't buy the Halloran hype. Plus, Seamus and I worked together at Boys State this summer and kind of bonded. We went out, found a bartender who didn't care how young we were, and had a few barley burgers. I got to know him a little. And McElroy's leg would have to be broken before he'd sit out a rivalry game."

***

A bright-eyed mid-20s Miss Riley does her best to concentrate on correcting papers while managing a restless Kennedy Elementary fourth-grade classroom, periodically looking up at her students to assure compliance and accountability. Her occasional and subtle glances toward the habitual offenders appropriately punctuate the desired message. As the period bell rings, she does her best to control the organized mayhem as her students gather their belongings, anxious for their next playground adventure. She calls out the name of a student, asking Mr. McElroy to join her before his exit.

From the back of the room, a bright-eyed young man with long, unkempt hair gingerly meanders up to his mentor's desk, his eyes not leaving the floor.

Miss Riley smiles, taking a deep breath. "How are you, Seamus?" The boy humbly, yet respectfully, replies, "I'm OK."

The teacher gently voices her concern over his well-being, recognizing his mother's passing several weeks earlier. Miss Riley eventually comments on young Mr. McElroy's interest and abilities on the playground, where he exhibits superior abilities while playing football with his classmates. She continues by describing a program that allows select Montana children to attend a college football game at the University of Montana in Missoula. She has spoken to his grandfather, who has agreed to allow him to travel the two hours by bus with a chaperone and other Butte students to a game the following weekend. The boy shows little emotion as he continues to wallow in his grief, not fully comprehending the extraordinary compassion of the young educator. She rises out of her chair and skirts her desk to give him a heartfelt hug. He accepts her embrace, returning his eyes to the rickety floor as his mind returns to his maternal thoughts.

Having never ventured outside of Silver Bow County, Seamus experiences mixed emotions that vacillate from apprehension to excitement as a yellow school bus pulls next to Dornblaser Stadium. The disadvantaged Mining City children press their noses against the windows as the festive tailgating fans attend to their respective pregame rituals. As the kids unload, they are greeted by large men, philanthropic-minded former university athletes who periodically donate their time and money to allow the less fortunate to attend the state's largest sporting event. After the children are provided with a meal and various sports paraphernalia, they are quickly whisked away to the southwest corner of the field, where the home team is congregating before running out onto the field. The youths silently marvel at the immense size of the players, some of whom reach out as they walk by to the outstretched hands of the newly branded, mesmerized fans. Little Seamus, appreciating the efforts of the generous alumni, manages his first smile in weeks as the players run onto the immaculate grass field.

***

Dr. Wells pulls into her driveway in Pattee Canyon, an upscale neighborhood in the hills above Missoula. Missoula, a small city nestled in the mountains of western Montana, is located in the center of the largest extinct lake in the history of the world. It was never a cowboy town; it was settled in the late 1800s by East Coast businessmen who did their best to make their brides comfortable in the remote western surroundings, importing deciduous trees from the Northeast. The architecture of downtown shows the Eastern influences from a century earlier. Home of the University of Montana, it's a college town and conservative Montana's liberal island. It's somewhat of a melting pot that refuses to melt.

The sky is streaked with light, and the air is chilly. Marianne huddles in her jacket as she grabs the paper from the mailbox, her hair still wet from a quick post-work shower. She drops her keys and purse in the front hall and walks into the kitchen, where she's met by the remains of her husband's breakfast: some half-eaten toast and a cup of coffee cooling on the island. She sets the paper by his plate, scans the headlines and takes a bite of his cold toast. Outside, a car door closes, and Marianne glances up to see her husband take off in his sporty black Audi. Marianne slides the rest of the toast into the trash and rinses his dishes. She rummages through the refrigerator for something more appetizing, but nothing looks good. She's tired, and her skeletons were rattled last night. Recently, sadness has become a symptom difficult to kick.

"Morning, Mama." Marianne's youngest, Polly, walks in dressed for school. She's wearing a vintage purple letterman's jacket embroidered with the name Sherman and a P in yellow on the front. "Long night?" Polly pours herself some cereal and settles in at the island next to her mother.

"I can't decide between coffee and a nap," Marianne says. "How did you sleep, sweetheart?" Polly gives a so-so hand signal with one hand as she chews her cereal, and Marianne reaches out to stroke her hair. "Anything you want to talk about?" Marianne says.

"I'm just stressing about that history test. Hey, so you and Dad are busy with his college friends for homecoming, right?"

"Well, I'm sure I could get out of it if you want me at the high school game," Marianne says.

"No, that's OK. I know it's a big deal for Dad," Polly says. "I just want fair warning so I'm not in the house when they show up."

Marianne laughs. "Oh, be nice. They're not that bad."

Polly rolls her eyes. "Go Griz!" she says with a big, fake cheerleader smile. "OK, I'm off." She puts her bowl in the dishwasher and gives her mother a kiss on the cheek. "If you talk to Colin today, tell him I'm sick of being an only child, and he needs to get his butt back here already."

Her daughter gone, Marianne deflates a bit. She trudges up the stairs to the bedroom, where she's greeted by her husband's clothes on the closet floor. After tossing them into the hamper, she picks up the last item, a rumpled button-down shirt. She breathes in its scent of cigars and perfume. A hotel key falls from the pocket. Marianne turns it over. She puts the shirt into the hamper and gingerly closes the lid. This is not the first time.

She dials her husband's cell phone. "Hi," she says to his voice mail. "It's me. Don't forget we have that appointment this afternoon. It's important, OK? Don't be late."

She goes to the bathroom window and leans her forehead against the cool glass. At the corner, Polly is waiting for the bus, talking to a boy Marianne doesn't recognize. The purple of her jacket stands out against the Missoula fall colors—pale yellowing hills, bright gold maples, and deep blue skies. Polly kicks at the downed leaves and laughs, happy.

***

Marianne quickly throws on a pair of jeans and Birkenstocks and ventures back downtown, heading to a bistro for weekly coffee with some of the girls. Then she'll return home for some shut-eye. As she walks into the bistro, she can already hear her group of friends cackling, led, of course, by the now 50-something Amanda, a financial consultant and Missoula socialite. Amanda is already on a roll and has the group in hysterics. Marianne cracks a smile as she gets closer to the table. Amanda stands and greets her best friend, giving her a hug and telling her, "You look like hell." She then asks Marianne about her night and her spirit, something Marianne's husband should have done 30 minutes earlier.

***

Welcome to Missoula County Stadium. It is a clear fall evening under the lights. The stadium is packed as two undefeated AA Montana high school football teams collide. In the raucous locker room, several Hellgate players tape steel rods under their arm pads, assuming the rugged mining kids from Butte will be doing the same. The scarlet-and-gold-adorned Knights football team rushes onto the field. On the other half of the field, the mighty Butte Bulldogs are an intimidating wall of white, purple, and gold. Brian throws passes to warm up as his teammates go through their final pregame drills and rituals. The coaches scan the field. Halloran calls the assistant head coach to his side and runs over the field conditions and the game plan, until finally, he comes to the key question: "Have you seen McElroy in the stands?" The assistant coach shrugs and shakes his head.

Halloran grins, cautious in his optimism, triple-checking the field and the stands for number 17. He signals his team to huddle up. The players are equally excited. Brian continues to watch but remains skeptical. Part of him was looking forward to playing against such a gifted athlete. As the pregame clock winds its way down to zero, the national anthem and color guard are ceremoniously performed, and the coin toss is completed.

The teams gather for final instructions and inspiration. The Hellgate crowd is pumped up. Brian walks toward the huddle. As he approaches his teammates, the visitors' section erupts, and without looking, Brian says, "Son of a bitch."

(*Ah! Leah! by Donnie Iris*)

With his long hair protruding from the bottom of his golden helmet, McElroy jogs onto the field, noticeably favoring a heavily taped leg, and greets his teammates.

The game is over before it starts. In front of several college scouts and the jubilant visitors from Butte, Seamus McElroy shakes off the injury and has the game of his high school career, playing both offense and defense. He is a man among boys this particular night. He punishes Brian, Steve, and every other player on the opposite side of the ball. A Hellgate linebacker, sporting the steel rods under his arm pads and constantly mouthing off, gets drilled by Seamus in front of the Hellgate bench. There is no dialogue from the star, just straight-up, hard-hitting football, most of the shots coming from the defensive side of the ball. His teammates take care of the taunting and intimidation factor. Seamus plays only three quarters. Butte wins 35–6. The Hellgate Knights' bubble has unceremoniously imploded.

Fans and families congregate on the field, cheering and consoling their respective teams. Brian is surrounded by Amanda, Marianne, and Brian's and Amanda's parents. "Hon, you're a mess. Let me get you some ice," Mrs. Callaghan says, pushing back her son's sweat-slicked hair to get a better look at his bruises.

Brian flicks his head away. "I'm fine, Mom."

"She's right, you know," Amanda says. "You don't want to look too tough." She hands him an ice pack, and he takes it.

"Callaghan!" A player in a soiled Butte jersey makes his way across to the group. Seamus takes off his helmet, revealing his face for the first time. Seamus is much larger than Brian and is strikingly handsome, with the long, feathered hair of the late 1970s. He shakes Brian's hand and gives him a brief hug. "Sorry about that," he says. "How you holdin' up?"

"Bum wheel, my ass!" Brian says, laughing.

Seamus, having taken off some of his pads in the fourth quarter, shows him a nasty leg bruise. "It's all heart, Lucky. All heart."

Amanda and Marianne are uncharacteristically quiet as Brian introduces Seamus to his parents and the Andersons and, finally, the girls. "This is my girlfriend, Amanda," Brian says, wanting to make their relationship clear. "And this is Marianne."

"Thanks for wearing Butte colors tonight, Marianne," Seamus says, checking out her prized letterman's jacket.

"It's Polson, actually," Amanda says.

"Sure, looks like Butte. Good enough for me," Seamus says. "Anyway, I'd better get back. It was nice meeting you all." He puts a hand on Brian's shoulder. "Take it easy, Lucky."

Brian gives Seamus an unappreciative stare as the star grins and jogs away.

"Lucky?" Amanda says.

"He's really not as funny as he thinks he is."

The trio watches Seamus nurse his sore leg as he crosses the field and eventually hugs an older man, presumably a relative.

"Sure, looks good walking away, though," Amanda whispers

to Marianne.

Brian grabs his bloody, muddy, sweat-covered towel from around his neck and tosses it at Amanda. "Here. Wipe that drool from your lip."

"Oh, ew, Brian, gross," Amanda says, flinging it back at him and giggling with Marianne.

Chapter 4

It is another gorgeous autumn Saturday morning in Butte. The world-famous Berkeley Pit, an immense open-pit copper mining operation, seems to stretch on forever. Dirt and rock have been carved hundreds of feet into the earth, with each terraced level revealing its own unique shades of brown, red and gray. Suddenly, an explosion rocks the mountain; debris flies everywhere. They are blasting this morning.

A group of men emerge from an outcropping: three older workers and, finally, behind them, Seamus. Seamus fills in for a shift now and then when work is available. The three men are Seamus's grandfather's friends—they've taken Seamus under their wing since Paddy was disabled several years earlier. They are surrogate fathers in a way and are proud of this young man. This morning, they're on his case about a tackle he missed in the second quarter of the last game. They know he's the best athlete to come out of Butte in decades, if not ever, but they're not about to let him rest on his laurels. Seamus can dish it as well as take it, but he's ready to get home. "All right, all right," Seamus says. "See you at the bar." He heads off toward his old red Chevy pickup. It's been a long shift.

On the way to his truck, a locomotive switch engine pulling ore cars passes in front of Seamus. His eyes twinkle with his passion for trains, and he runs to hop into the cab with another old friend of Paddy's. After a short ride, he jumps down near where he's parked, hard hat and gloves in hand. As he reaches for the truck's door handle, Seamus's eye catches a reflection on the ground. He bends down and picks up a valueless piece of quartz that somewhat resembles a large diamond. Knowing the stone's innate value, he examines the crystal before placing it in the truck's ashtray. After the red truck grinds to an eventual start, Seamus slips a cassette into a tape player and drives the beat-up Chevy home as the music blares.

(*Peace of Mind by Boston*)

Seamus lives with his maternal grandfather, Paddy, a jolly, overweight 60-something bar owner who walks with a limp from a mining accident—his badge of courage of sorts. Their home is simple, but has real character, much like Paddy. It's not upscale by any means but is nice for the two bachelors. Seamus showers, grabs a leftover sandwich, glances at the local paper's sports page, and then heads down to his grandfather's pub to tend bar and complete other duties assigned by the patriarch.

The Irish pub is packed with Saturday night patrons who are excited to see the high school star. As always, Paddy is the life of the party. Seamus catches familiar snippets of his grandfather's bar wit and wisdom drifting over the noise in the room: Paddy's telling a customer about "growing up so poor we couldn't even pay attention." He tells a woman who has just arrived, "Belly up, and let me introduce you to my friend Dr. Al K. Hall." Paddy will talk anyone's ear off on any subject, and he's got sage advice for anyone willing to listen. He pivots from the new customer back to the first one, picking up where he left off. "Bullshit and backstabbing will only get a person so far. After that, it's hard work and integrity."

Seamus slips behind the bar and ties on an apron.

"Well, look who finally showed up," Paddy says. He grabs the newspaper and gestures to the restroom. "See ya in a few. I've got to drop the kids off at the pool."

The new woman is less than impressed.

The night wears on. Seamus laughs, pours beer, tends the grill, waits on the customers, jokes with the locals, and teases the regulars' wives. A new patron asks about two old black-and-white framed photographs behind the bar, one of Paddy in a U.S. Navy uniform and the other a weathered picture of a group of miners. The regulars roll their eyes, joking about "the story that keeps on giving." Paddy shuts up his regulars with a condescending remark, happily pointing to the picture of himself serving on the deck of an American aircraft carrier in the 1940s, and then to the miners working in a Chilean mine in the early 1900s. He points out his father, Seamus's great-grandfather, who worked for the Anaconda Copper Company in northern Chile before coming to Montana. Paddy explains the connection between the South American mines in the Andes Mountains and Anaconda Copper's interests in the northern Rocky Mountains. His patrons eventually begin to heckle him; he tells them to piss off. The immigrant miners' piercing eyes stare out from the weathered photograph at the festive bar scene.

The fine autumn day is long gone. Paddy goes to the window and says, "Rainin' like a cow pissin' on a flat rock."

One of the patrons calls him back with a complaint about a warm beer.

"Oh, stop squallin' like a mashed cat, and mind your pints and quarts," Paddy says.

Seamus makes his way over to a table where a half-eaten hot-pepper cheeseburger remains and clears the refuse. Back at the grill, he flips two beef patties onto their respective buns and places the sizzling burgers on a clean plate with the half-eaten leftover. He sneaks a look at Paddy before grabbing a couple of beers from the cooler and then heads out the back door leading to the alley. The storm has passed, but the street is wet, and the air is heavy. He veers around the dumpster and finds two homeless men huddled between two buildings. "Evening, Bob. Evening, James," Seamus says. "Sorry it's got to be a quick one—Paddy's got his eye on me." He hands over this week's feast and then stoops to feed the leftover burger to their scraggly dog.

The men thank him.

"See you next week," Seamus calls, disappearing back behind the heavy metal door to the pub. He tries to slip back to his post, only to catch a disapproving glance from Paddy. Seamus quickly asks a couple customers if he can refill their drinks, and Paddy turns to some friends, cracking a gentle smile of approval. He knows he's raising Seamus right.

***

The next morning, Paddy is up around nine o'clock and in tough shape, nursing a bad hangover. He shuffles to the kitchen, trying to sweep out the cobwebs. "Good soul," he says, pouring himself a cup of Seamus's home-brewed coffee. He finds his readers, scans a note left by his grandson, and eventually picks up the paper. Adjusting his privates, he sits down.

Seamus is long gone.

(*Come Monday by Jimmy Buffett*)

Sunday is his day off. He attended Father Matule's early Mass and headed up the Big Hole Valley to fly-fish and hunt grouse. Paddy owns a modest cabin on 120 acres there, which he purchased from some old prospector decades earlier. Paddy uses it as his elk-hunting cabin and hideaway, a refuge that heals and feeds the soul. He keeps horses and kicks back by building fences and working on menial projects when he wants to escape his daily routine. As a young boy, Seamus spent countless hours picking rocks out of the field and moving irrigation pipe. This is where Paddy taught his grandson his work ethic.

The Big Hole Valley is spectacular: an enormous stretch of flat green land braided by rivers and creeks with cottonwoods and willows blazing on their banks and hemmed in by the sharp rise of mountains. Seamus enjoys another fantastic champagne fall day accompanied by his beloved dog, Angus, a massive and regal black Labrador Retriever. While Seamus fishes, Angus stalks and chases grasshoppers and frogs, dives for rocks, flushes birds, nips at Seamus's fish, and rolls in the grass. Angus falls asleep on his back with a chewed-up stick in his mouth and his legs straight up in the air, making Seamus laugh. Seamus joins him for a Sunday afternoon nap.

In the evening, Seamus returns home with several nice fish and a couple of grouse. Paddy's in the kitchen, fixing supper. "Have a good time killing minnows and ground-sluicing grouse?" Paddy says, looking over his grandson's catch.

"Have a good time missing Mass and a beautiful day of cast-and-blast in the valley, you old lush?" Seamus says. "You know what else you missed? Ole Widow Molloy was asking about you at church. Made you a rhubarb pie."

"Why the hell would any human being eat something that every neighborhood dog pees on?"

Paddy hands him a bowl of chili, and Seamus heads to the living room. He kicks off his shoes, turns on the TV, and sinks into the couch. Seamus takes a bite and winces. "You wanna warn me next time you hand me a bowl of boiling hot sauce? What'd you put in here?"

Paddy yells back from the kitchen, "Quit your behavin', and learn how to don't!"

"Someday, you have to tell me what the hell that means."

Later that evening, Seamus is in his bedroom, studying. Paddy comes in, dishrag in hand, looking every inch a bartender.

"You do any thinking today about those college options?"

Seamus puts down his pencil. He's getting a little tired of this conversation. He's entertained scholarship offers from more than 15 schools already, including several Pac-10 schools and both the University of Montana and Montana State. One school, and only one school, is on Paddy's Irish mind: Notre Dame. Notre Dame sent a letter of interest during the summer and had a scout out in the early fall, and Paddy checks the mailbox daily for an offer letter. This would be heavenly for Paddy, a grandfather in an Irish Catholic mining town, but he won't mention it directly. Still, Seamus knows what he's driving at with his roundabout college questions.

"No big news," Seamus says. He's more interested in playing the game, getting an education, and staying in the West. He wants to study environmental and mining engineering as well as business, and he's not sure Notre Dame's the place for that. "Don't worry; we still have plenty of time. But don't go pinning all your hopes on Notre Dame—you know they wanted a little faster 40."

Paddy flips his hand, discounting the coaches' comment. He looks up at a Heart poster on the wall, taking in the Wilson sisters. "Well, I'll see myself out. You let me know if you want to talk it over," he says. He nods at the poster. "Give a poor ole man a goddamn heart attack."

Seamus shakes his head and picks up his pencil again.

***

That same evening, Amanda and Marianne are procrastinating at the Anderson home. They're on the floor in Amanda's room with their backs up against the bed and their books spread around them.

"So, what do you and Steve want to do before the Sadie Hawkins dance? Or, more importantly, after?"

Marianne flips the pages of her physics textbook. "I didn't actually ask him. Steve's fine and everything—I just don't know. He's always sort of leering at me, you know? I feel like dinner."

Amanda laughs. "For someone so relatively popular, you'd

think he'd be able to keep it together a little better. You got someone else in mind?"

"I'm just not really interested in dating. I don't think I'm really ready."

Amanda nods and opens her French notebook. "OK, cherie," she says. She never knows where or when this darkness is going to show up, but when she hears that tone of voice, she knows to back off.

Marianne begins an equation and then sets her pencil down. "You think that Butte guy might be willing to travel to Missoula?"

Amanda gasps. "Well, well. Only the best for Miss Sherman."

"Oh, please. I thought he seemed like a nice guy—that's all."

"He probably has a girlfriend in Butte—hell, several girlfriends in Butte—and you know what those girls are like." Amanda looks at Marianne, who looks more crestfallen than she'd been shooting for. "What the heck? The worst he can do is say no." Amanda scoots up off the ground and crosses to the phone on the dresser. She dials directory assistance for his number, tries several McElroys before finding success, and then passes Marianne the phone.

Marianne is startled when Paddy answers. She nearly hangs up, but Amanda catches her hand and puts the phone back to her ear.

Paddy, for his part, is used to girls calling for Seamus, but a long-distance call is something new. Paddy calls Seamus to the phone, and as soon as Seamus sees the grin on Paddy's face, he knows he's in for a ribbing.

"Hello?" Seamus cups his hand over the phone and waves Paddy off. There's a pause, and he hears some muffled sounds over the line. "Hello?"

"Hi. Seamus? This is Marianne Sherman, Brian Callaghan's friend. From Missoula. We met at the game last week."

"I remember. Polson colors. Hi."

"So, I know this is out of the blue, and I'm really sorry to bother you like this, but we have this Sadie Hawkins dance next Saturday. You know, we have to dress up and everything, and it's kind of dumb but also kind of fun. I'm going with Brian and Amanda, and I was wondering if you wanted to come with me. I mean, to be my date."

Seamus is caught off guard. Before he can answer, Marianne

continues, obviously embarrassed. "I know it's far away. It's no big deal."

"No, no, that'd be great. Sorry. I was just thinking—I normally work Saturdays, but I'm sure I can swing it. So yeah. I love an adventure."

"Oh. Great." There's another muffled pause, and then Marianne's back on the line. "Brian's going to give you a call with directions to his house. Six o'clock?"

As soon as the phone hits the cradle, Paddy's back in the room, eyes twinkling, eyebrows raised. "Missoula, huh? Far way to go just to chase skirt and get in trouble."

Seamus backs out of the kitchen, his left ring finger up as if to flip Paddy off. "You're not worth the big one."

∗∗∗

The following Saturday afternoon, Seamus frantically rushes through errands, confidently fielding colorful comments and prodding from Paddy and his bar cronies. Seamus pulls up at Brian's parents' house, music blaring from the cassette player of the beat-up Chevy.

(*Roll on Down the Highway by Bachman Turner Overdrive*)

The Callaghan home is a large, beautiful home in an old and affluent part of town. Huge maples line the streets; each house sits surrounded by a skirt of well-tended lawn. Seamus is the closest to intimidated that he's been in a long time—he had no idea places like this even existed in Montana. He checks himself in the rearview mirror and then heads up the broad front steps. Mr. Callaghan answers the door. Brian's close behind, trying to avoid what he knows is coming. His dad played football at the University of Montana and is a huge Seamus fan.

"Seamus McElroy. It is a true pleasure." Mr. Callaghan shakes Seamus's hand with unnecessary vigor.

"Good to see you again, Mr. Callaghan," Seamus says. "You too, Lucky."

"Oh, hey now, I've been spending some serious time on the squat rack at the gym," Brian says.

Mr. Callaghan looks lost at the boys' inside joke. He puts a hand on Seamus's shoulder and guides him to the kitchen, where Mrs. Callaghan is chopping mushrooms for dinner.

"So, Seamus, I bet those scouts can't get enough of you. Fill me in. Who have you been talking to? You leanin' any particular direction?"

"Dad," Brian says. "Please." He shoots his mom a desperate look. She wipes her hands on her apron and comes around the kitchen island.

Mr. Callaghan plows right on. "You know, U of M may not be the conventional choice, but I gotta tell you, we're shaping up to be one hell of a program."

"Hon," Mrs. Callaghan says, "let the poor boy be. Seamus, it's nice to see you again."

"Nice to see you too, Mrs. Callaghan," Seamus says. He doesn't want to be rude to Mr. Callaghan, though, so he turns back to him. "You know, I'd love to stay close to home. Might not make the most sense football-wise, but I'd rather not leave Montana. Problem is, they don't offer a degree in engineering."

Mr. Callaghan looks temporarily deflated. "Well, I am sure sorry to hear that. I guess I'll just count myself lucky you're not planning to be a Cat next year." Montana State, the agricultural school over in Bozeman, is the U of M Grizzlies' fiercest rival. Mr. Callaghan extends his hand with his fingers pointing toward the ground and pulls downward on the fingers as if they're nipples on an udder—the MSU handshake. Seamus chuckles politely. Mrs. Callaghan finally puts her foot down.

"Well, that is more than enough shop talk," she says. "You boys had better get dressed, or you'll be late, and Amanda will have your heads. And, Seamus," she calls as the boys head upstairs, "take better care of my son than you did last month."

The Andersons live across the Clark Fork River in another well-off neighborhood. Their house is more modern, with big glass windows looking out at Mount Jumbo and, in the distance, the Rattlesnake Wilderness. The boys sit in the living room, trying to make small talk with Dr. and Mrs. Anderson and feeling a bit silly in their Li'l Abner overalls and ripped shirts.

The girls finally make their grand entrance in matching Daisy Mae outfits, Amanda twirling to show off her clothing and

Marianne looking a little shy in her low-cut blouse. Marianne almost never wears skirts—she's a tomboy through and through—and tonight she's a knockout. Even Brian is having a hard time keeping his eyes on Amanda. Amanda leans over and whispers in his ear, "Mine aren't as big, but they'll poke your eyes out." He looks sheepish, and she continues, louder this time. "Now, tell me all about what a great job I did with Marianne's hair. Doesn't she look amazing?" She may play jealous, but Amanda's basically just thrilled that Marianne agreed to come out.

The night is filled with laughter, dancing, photographs, and checking out the crowd. Brian and Seamus sneak a drink or two, but it's all fairly innocent. Seamus and Marianne share a slow dance, and it's clear to both that there's a spark between them.

(*I'm In You by Peter Frampton*)

After the dance, the four head up to the woods to a kegger with some friends. It's fun up there, but before long, the four of them realize they'd rather just be on their own. "Let's go back to your place," Amanda says to Brian. She rounds up Marianne and Seamus, and everyone piles into Brian's car. "To the Missoula Hilton!"

On the way out of the campground, Brian high-centers his car on a levy next to a small irrigation ditch.

"Oh, for Christ's sake, Brian," Amanda says. "If you're gonna insist on driving all the time, you should learn to goddamn drive. Out, out, out." Amanda slides across to the driver's seat while the others bail out to push. Even in her skirt, Marianne's game to help out. Finally, they push the car free and drive to Brian's house, where they make popcorn and hot chocolate to warm up. Marianne's gamble paid off this night.

Amanda conveniently whisks Brian away, leaving Marianne and Seamus in the kitchen to talk. They've been at each other's side all night, but it's the first time they've been alone together, and for a moment, neither is sure what to say.

"So, do you know what you're doing next year?" Seamus asks.

"I'm sticking around here. I got some really great academic scholarships, so I can actually afford it. I mean, I have a little money but I wasn't sure I'd be able to go." Marianne flushes, uncomfortable at having brought the conversation into such a personal place. "I'm sorry—I didn't mean to make things so serious."

Seamus watches her pressing her hands around her mug. "Do you mind my asking what happened?"

"There was a car wreck. It was four years ago now—my parents and my sister were killed. I just broke my leg. I lived with my grandmother for a couple years, and then she passed and …" Marianne trails off. She's not used to saying any of this out loud. "Anyway, the Andersons were my parents' best friends, and they took me in. They're pretty incredible, actually. I don't know if you got to talk to them at all today."

Seamus recognizes her stab at redirecting the conversation. He can see how tense she is. "We didn't really get beyond hello, but I'll take your word for it." He pauses. "It's rare, meeting someone whose life has also had some ups and downs and who's willing to talk about it."

Marianne looks up.

"I live with my grandfather. I think you two talked on the phone the other week. Sorry if he was rude."

Marianne laughs and shakes her head. "He wasn't rude."

"Well, that's a first. My mom died when I was little. Breast cancer. And who knows who my dad was? Some transient miner. So now it's just me and Paddy. I bet you'd get a kick out of him." Seamus describes living in the Mining City, telling funny bar stories, until Amanda and Marianne have to go home. He's not going to push Marianne, and she can tell. Marianne is surprised at how comfortable she is with him; she's found someone she can relate to, though Seamus is further along in the healing process.

Back in Butte, Seamus is preoccupied at the bar and at home. He can't stop thinking about Marianne. He realizes he has met someone like him, someone who has endured loss far too early in life. Paddy notices the change but is wise enough to let it run its course. He shakes his head and complains to his cronies about his teenager's growing pains.

Chapter 5

They don't see each other again until February. Seamus's football season takes off; Butte wins the state championship, and Seamus takes home the state MVP award. Seamus stays busy studying, working out, and helping at the bar, church, and mine. He hunts elk with Paddy and his cronies near the spectacular Big Hole River ranch. Seamus's ranch days are a blur of chopping wood, dressing a harvested bull elk, and taking care of the packhorses. As fall moves into winter, the valley is breathtaking. The Pintler Mountain Range whitens under intense blue skies, and waters are low and still. The solitude of the ranch lies in sharp contrast to Seamus's busy life back in Butte.

Things are quieter in Missoula. Marianne's basketball career comes to an early end as her team loses a divisional game in Missoula. She's sad that it's all over. She accepts her Hellgate letter with pride at her team banquet and receives a scarlet-and-gold jacket from Dr. Anderson as a celebratory gift. She spends the holidays with Amanda and her family for the first time. Dr. and Mrs. Anderson take special care to make sure she feels included, but the holidays are particularly hard for Marianne. For her part, Amanda keeps trying to set Marianne up on dates. Finally, when it's clear that despite all Marianne's excuses, Amanda's going to keep on going, Marianne tells her she had a bad dating experience. It's all she needs to say: Amanda is intuitive enough not to go down that road.

Winter rolls along with a routine series of tests, parties, and basketball games. One bitterly cold Friday night, the Butte boys' basketball team is in town. Midway through the second quarter, Seamus saunters into the gym with a couple of University of Montana football coaches. The coaches are recruiting Seamus heavily, even though UM is much less prestigious than the Pac-10 schools, let alone Notre Dame, and they know they can't offer him his preferred major.

Seamus turns heads when he enters. He's sporting his highly decorated letterman's jacket, Levi 501s, and cowboy boots. Steve elbows Brian, who turns and says, "Well, shit."

On Brian's other side, Amanda is in the middle of a story. When it becomes clear he's no longer listening, she waves her hand in front of his face. "I don't talk for my own entertainment, you know. Who's so important you can't listen to your own girlfriend? Some nice, well-bred Butte girl?"

"On the contrary," said Brian. Put your bib on—your stud boyfriend from Butte showed up with the Griz coaches."

Amanda nudges Marianne, and they watch Seamus head for the Butte booster section. He stands with the university coaches, shaking hands with the visiting Butte parents and students. At halftime, Seamus spots Brian in the crowd and makes his way over to the Missoula group.

Despite their fledgling friendship, Brian is still a little star struck. He's elated to have the state's football MVP coming over to chat with him, and he's equally chagrined when Seamus greets him as Lucky yet again. Seamus says hi to Amanda and Marianne and then gets sucked into a conversation with Brian about college prospects. The girls try to play it cool, but they're obviously gawking.

Seamus sits down next to Marianne. "I was hoping you'd be here," Seamus says. "I'm sorry I haven't been in touch—things got pretty crazy the past couple months."

"Me too," Marianne says. "I mean, things have been super busy here also." She fidgets, excited. "Not as busy as a state championship, though. That's amazing—congratulations." She sees him glancing back at the UM coaches and takes a breath, figuring it's her one shot. "So, um, I figure you probably have stuff going on tonight, but a bunch of us are going to a party on the South Hill after the game."

Seamus is once again caught off guard by Marianne's mix of shyness and directness. "That sounds a hell of a lot better than whatever I'm supposed to be doing," he says. "I'm staying in the dorms, but I'm pretty sure I can sneak out. I'll work it out with Brian—it'll be like Boys State."

The second half of the basketball game begins, and Seamus returns to the coaches. Seamus catches Marianne watching him as he crosses the floor. He tips his Coca-Cola cup in her direction, and she quickly looks away, embarrassed.

Amanda says, "Did I just hear you ask Seamus McElroy out on another date?"

"It's not a date," Marianne says. "I bet Brian would've invited him anyway."

"Speaking of which," Amanda says as she turns to Brian, "I'm dying of suspense. What's going on with the whole 'Lucky' thing?"

"It's nothing. At Boys State, Seamus gave me crap about my skinny legs and said they're lucky legs—lucky they don't break in half and stab me in the ass. That Butte rat is a real sack of shit."

Amanda and Marianne crack up.

Brian parks his emerald-green 1972 Camaro in front of the party, aware they make a good picture piling out of the car. Seamus is up front, and Amanda, Marianne, and Steve are crammed together in the back. Half the student body must be at this party. It's a typical parents-out-of-town event: keg in the bathtub, Rainier beer in the kitchen sink, guys eating Twinkies with mustard, spiked punch in the kitchen, potato chips everywhere, and the stereo blaring.

(*Jet Airliner by Steve Miller Band*)

The boys make the rounds, introducing Seamus to all their friends. "If Brian ever stops swooning, we'll have dates again, but until then, looks like we're on our own," Amanda says.

The boys eventually make it back to them, and Marianne and Seamus chat. He tells her he's still hoping for a letter from Notre Dame, even though it isn't his first choice. He explains that being a member of the Fighting Irish is his grandfather's dream for him.

The party starts to get rowdy, with beer bongs, games of quarters, dancing, eggs exploding in the microwave, and more good, clean fun. Suddenly, there's a knock at the door: it's the police, followed 20 seconds later by the parents returning early from their ski vacation. Brian grabs Amanda and yells to Seamus, "Let's get out of here!"

(*Get Up and Enjoy Yourself by Head East*)

Seamus grabs Marianne's hand, and they head out the back door and run through the neighborhood, laughing and out of breath. They hide in some bushes until they have a chance to get to Brian's car. Steve speeds by in someone else's passenger seat. When the coast seems relatively clear, they spring for Brian's car. Amanda jumps in last through the open passenger window and slams the gearshift into drive while her legs dangle out of the car.

They settle down, joking around as they cruise Missoula. At a stoplight, two guys in a jacked-up truck begin to chase them, revving their engine and flashing their brights. They eventually pull up to the side of the Camaro, goofing off to get Amanda's attention. Annoyed, she rolls down her window and holds up her hand with her thumb and forefinger an inch apart, suggesting the size of their respective manhood. She rolls up the window and turns back to Brian. "Well, I think that message went through loud and clear," she says, pleased with herself.

They eventually drop Seamus back at the dorm, and he thanks the three of them and invites them to stop by his granddad's pub if they ever make it to Butte.

***

On a Tuesday one week before National Letter of Intent day, Seamus comes home from his after-school workout to find the long-awaited Notre Dame letter. He runs a finger across the embossed envelope, noting the South Bend, Indiana, postmark. He drops the remaining mail on the entryway table, walks through the house, retrieves Angus from the backyard, and heads down the street to the neighborhood outdoor ice-skating rink. The rink is busy with families enjoying evening skating. Children laugh and shriek. He sits on the edge of the rink, contemplating the decision in his hand. He takes a breath and opens the envelope.

He has been accepted, offered a partial academic scholarship, and asked to walk on to the Notre Dame football team. It is not what he had hoped for, but it will be enough for Paddy.

Angus whines and noses Seamus's knee, wanting him to throw snowballs for him; Seamus obliges. He looks back at the letter, rereading it, and then looks into space. Seamus gets up and walks around the neighborhood, eventually ending up at Paddy's pub. Paddy is working the bar and bullshitting with some of the regulars. "Seamus!" he says, grinning. "You want a double whiskey ditch?"

Seamus declines and smiles. "Do you have a minute?"

Paddy glances at Seamus, a bit surprised. "Frankie," he says, "man the bar, would you? And you're not to be giving away any freebies, goddammit." He pushes himself up and rambles to the bar's office behind the Montana stud poker table.

Seamus follows and closes the office door before handing Paddy the letter. Paddy looks up with a little mist in his eyes. Paddy reads the letter over again, wipes his eyes, and hugs his grandson. "What are you waiting for? Let's go celebrate, boy!"

Seamus expected this response, but is less than enthused. Paddy sees the look on his face and eases back into his chair.

"I know this is what you want for me, but think about it. It's only a partial academic scholarship—it doesn't guarantee a spot on the team, and I want to play football."

"Seamus, this is not even up for discussion. This is what you've been working for. And once they see you on the field, once they see how hard you work, they'll give you that athletic scholarship." Paddy shakes the letter at Seamus. "What the hell are you thinking?"

Seamus pauses. "I've made my decision. I'm going to the University of Montana."

Paddy cannot believe what he has just heard. Seamus has seen Paddy in a rage before, but this is the first time his grandfather's Irish temper has been aimed at him. Paddy shouts that the U of M doesn't even have the major Seamus wants to pursue. They've been over this a million times: the school does have a good business school, but Paddy is adamant that Seamus should get the engineering degree first and then move on to an MBA program.

Seamus tries to keep his voice reasonable. "It's close to home. I can fish, I can hunt, and I can still do all the things I love—it's a place where I feel comfortable. And it's a full-ride athletic scholarship. It may not be Pac-10, but it's up-and-coming, and it's available right now. I can probably play next year or maybe after a redshirt season."

"Bullshit! Quit pissing in my ear and telling me it's raining!" Paddy slams his palms against the desk. "You're throwing away Notre Dame for some commie-pinko fag institution. All they do in Missoula is smoke the devil's lettuce and march in goddamn peace rallies. If you're so dead set on staying in state, why not MSU? At least they have a goddamn engineering school—or, hell, Montana Tech. You wouldn't even have to leave the house."

There is a long pause. Seamus slowly raises his head, his steely, confident, and razor-focused gaze squarely upon his beloved mentor. "They gave me a ticket to a game."

The aura in the cramped office abruptly changes. The patriarch's irrational anger momentarily subsides as he recognizes the true origin of the boy's logic while feeling the sharp edge of his only daughter's haunting memory. He points a finger at Seamus. "We will discuss this later, you damn fool." Paddy's tone and manner bring a growl from Angus, to which Paddy responds, "Get that son of a bitch out of my sight before I sell him to the Chinese restaurant across the street."

Seamus makes the long walk from the office to the bar door, past the silent gauntlet of customers he knows have heard every word of Paddy's meltdown. Behind him, Paddy pours himself a shot, a prelude to getting drunk. Seamus walks home with Angus, sad to have disappointed his grandfather. He looks at the letter one more time before putting it away in his worn jacket.

Later that evening, Paddy stumbles home. Deep down, he realizes Notre Dame is his dream, not Seamus's, and he's more hurt than angry. He shakes Seamus awake and tells his grandson he loves him and will support any decision he makes. "I'm glad to hear I'll have my fishing partner so close to home. And this way, I can catch all the games." He gives Seamus a big hug. "You know I'm proud of you, my boy."

***

Marianne spends her summer waiting tables at a Missoula restaurant. She and Amanda venture up to the Andersons' Flathead Lake cabin when they both have time off. Sometimes Dr. and Mrs. Anderson and Amanda's older brothers come with them, but most often, it's just the two girls. They spend quiet days together, fishing and hiking nearby, boating, and lying out with books on the dock. The lake stretches on around them, clear to its depths, mirroring the mountains around it. Flathead Lake brings out mixed emotions for Marianne—there's nowhere her family feels more alive to her.

Seamus works in southwestern Montana, spending most of his time haying on a large ranch in the Big Hole River Valley. It's hot and dirty work. Under a particularly fierce sun, Seamus rides the swather down the hay field, daydreaming. He wears his summer uniform: a sleeveless shirt, blue jeans, boots, and a straw cowboy hat. Every so often, he jumps down to check the machinery, but the monotone hum of the diesel engine has nearly lulled him to sleep. Suddenly, a tremendous sound rocks the Big Hole Valley. An F-16 fighter jet screams directly over Seamus's head: U.S. Air Force pilots from Great Falls' Malmstrom Air Force Base are buzzin' the Big Hole again. The deafening sound scares the hell out of Seamus, even though this is hardly the first time he's had this encounter. Seamus turns the machine off and stands up on his tractor, swearing and flipping off the pilot. In the commotion, his hat falls to the ground; he jumps down to retrieve it and sits back down on the tractor. He watches the lone pilot as he circles the valley, flying once again over Seamus. The pilot dips the plane's wings at Seamus as he heads back home east of the Continental Divide. Seamus smiles and waves, watching with amazement as the jet fighter clears the horizon. A sudden memory overwhelms him, and Seamus bows his head, his eyes welling.

He takes a break on a hay bale, alone in the middle of the huge field save for a hawk circling above. As Seamus eats his lunch, he watches the hawk swoop down to catch his lunch, a field mouse. At the end of his long day, he hits the local watering holes with the other ranch hands, jitterbugging with the local ranchers' daughters.

(*Livingston Saturday Night by Jimmy Buffett*)

Van Blakely

Chapter 6

(*Working Again by the Michael Stanley Band*)

Fall quarter begins at the University of Montana in Missoula. Seamus arrived early for football practice. He pays his dues, going through the normal hazing by upperclassmen. He is surprisingly strong, fast, smart, and eager to learn; he shows definitive leadership qualities and is never intimidated. Both senior classmen and coaches recognize his talent. The coaches debate redshirting him; they want him to fill out physically as much as possible. They realize he's a true professional prospect, something seldom seen coming out of Montana.

Meanwhile, the Missoula crew starts classes. Amanda talks Marianne into going through sorority rush even though Marianne doesn't think it seems like a good fit. The girls eventually pledge a sorority and get involved in the Greek system. Brian chooses to go the independent route.

Early in the semester, Marianne finds herself alone at a fraternity-sorority Hawaiian luau mixer. (*Thunder Island by Jay Ferguson*) Amanda, usually right by her side, has other plans and can't make it. The party is loud and filled with people Marianne doesn't know. An upperclassman in a Hawaiian shirt comes over and asks if he can get her a drink. He hands her a cup full to the brim with the lethal Hawaiian Punch/Everclear concoction they're serving. Nervous, she drinks. The punch is sweet and goes down fast.

The upperclassman, whose name she can't keep in her mind, invites her upstairs, and Marianne dizzily follows him to his bedroom. She sits on the edge of the bed, the room spinning around her. The boy makes some dumb jokes, and Marianne laughs. It's a little exciting—it's been awhile since she was this close to a boy, and his interest feels good. He moves in for a kiss. Marianne feels a little outside her body, but the kissing is nice enough. Maybe this is how college will be: parties, boys, and fun. Marianne is unconcerned and at ease, until the boy pushes her onto her back and fumbles at the front of her jeans. Marianne freezes. One hand mashes at her breast.

"Whoa, too fast," she says. She squirms and tries to sit up. He keeps going, trying to work the buttons of her fly. He's got a good 50 pounds on her. She can't remember his name. "Stop!" she says, louder this time. All Marianne can feel is the adrenaline surging. She presses her heels down, trying to find some leverage, and shoves him off her. "I told you to stop," she says. "What is wrong with you?"

He gets up, smoothing his hair. "Fucking cock tease," he says, and he slams the door as he leaves.

Marianne takes a moment to pull herself together. She walks out of the room and finds her way back to the staircase. She's aware of eyes on her from the living room below but myopically focuses on her exit, purposely not making eye contact with anyone. Three frat brothers watch her make her way down the stairs and toward the front door. She's obviously disoriented, her blouse untucked and wrinkled and her hair in disarray. The best-looking of the three, Andrew, gives a loud whistle. Andrew is tall and trim, with dark blond hair and a self-satisfied swagger. When Marianne's assailant joins the group, Andrew claps him on the shoulder. "Swing and a miss, huh? Shame you couldn't close the deal."

The youngest in the group, a recent pledge, watches Marianne try to keep her feet and pull open the heavy wooden door. "Check her out. Man, she is wasted."

The kid shrugs. "Party's a bust. Let's go downtown and play hogger."

"Hogger?" the pledge says. "What's that?"

"We pick a bar; we find the fattest, ugliest chicks; and we score. A fine traditional pastime."

Andrew calls to Marianne, still struggling with the door, "Having trouble, sweetheart?"

Marianne gets the door unstuck and makes it outside, where she promptly throws up.

The next morning, she wakes up in her bed with no memory of how she got there. There's a garbage can next to her bed, and she's spent a good portion of the night with the bottle flu. Amanda's bed is neatly made; she must have slept at Brian's. Marianne drags herself out of bed and looks at herself in the mirror. She presses her cold hands against her overheated skin. Memories of the night before rush back. She sits down on her bed and shuts her eyes, doing her best to keep the lid on the Pandora's box that last night opened.

***

In an emergency room, Dr. Wells looks intently at a patient's chart before asking two police officers if there is any other information she should know. They both shake their heads. The female patient looks at the door with a quiet desperation. Dr. Wells sets down the clipboard and takes the patient's hand, holding it as she explains the legal and health procedures for examining a rape victim. As Marianne begins her examination, she takes note of her own stress of again empathizing with a rape victim's state of mind, thinking to herself, Wow, twice in one week.

***

Over several weeks, Marianne withdraws within herself, struggling with the memories that have been stirred. Amanda notices the change, but as usual, she doesn't press her. Amanda knows there are parts of Marianne's past that she's not ready to share—she can only hope she will do so when the time is right.

Marianne makes her world smaller, spending most of her time running, working out, attending class, and studying. She maintains her pledge status mainly to appease Amanda. She feels alone.

At one of the many Greek functions, Andrew introduces himself to Marianne. He's a couple of years older, comes from a wealthy Seattle family, and is the stereotypical frat rat: he's spent his time in college chasing girls, drinking, experimenting with drugs, cheating in school, and manipulating every situation for his own benefit. There's something about Marianne, though, that he hasn't been able to get out of his head since the luau party—something about the way she carried herself in such a shitty situation. Tonight, she's cordial, and he's relieved she doesn't seem to remember him. He makes small talk, angling for a laugh. Marianne does her best to be social—he seems perfectly nice—but finally tells him she's heading home early to study.

"Admirable," he says. "Can I get your number at least?"

"Oh, I'm sure you'll see me at the next one of these things," she says.

"Right," he says. "See you around." Andrew's never been turned down so blatantly. He watches her disappear, intrigued.

The next week, the sorority house throws a Screw-Your-Roommate Dinner, for which each girl lines up a date for a fellow sorority sister. Marianne begs Amanda not to set her up; she says she'll be happy going stag. As the young men begin to fill the house, Marianne recognizes Andrew among the crowd, but she remains aloof. With a shudder, she notices her would-be rapist at his side. What the hell is he doing with him? Marianne grabs her bag, ready to head back to the dorm.

Amanda approaches and drapes an arm around her. "Oh, stick around at least till Brian gets here. He's bummed he hasn't seen you in so long." She pulls back and surveys Marianne's outfit. "Besides, you don't want to waste that top on your books. You look good."

Right on cue, Brian walks in the door. Marianne's heart begins to pound, and she struggles to hide her first smile in weeks: Seamus McElroy is at his side. The sorority is aflutter. Who is this large, handsome mystery guy? Marianne had forgotten how attracted she was to Seamus and how connected to him she felt. Plus, she can't help but feel flattered by the stir he's causing among her newfound friends. Brian and Seamus work their way across the room until they reach Amanda and Marianne.

"Hey, Polson," Seamus says. "Been awhile."

"Hi, Seamus," Marianne says, dropping her eyes. She's shy at first, but Seamus teases her until she begins to find her old self. He's fully aware of, but ignores, the attention from the other girls. They laugh and tell stories, continuing where they left off the previous winter. Amanda has come through. She is indeed Marianne's champion.

Chapter 7

Seamus and Marianne begin to date, falling in love fast. Seamus is not on the football team's travel squad and will be redshirted, which is fine with him, as his only real interest is now Marianne, his first true love. One night, after an evening with Brian and Amanda and a few drinks, Seamus and Marianne head back to her dorm room. They make out, but as usual, when things get too heavy, Marianne pulls back. Seamus sits up and takes her hand. He knows that something is haunting her. "What would you think about me staying over one of these nights?" he says.

It's so quiet that it takes him a second to realize Marianne is shaking with suppressed sobs. He hugs her close as she breaks down. She begins to calm down. "I've had some bad experiences," she says.

"I'm so sorry, Marianne," he says. "I didn't mean to push. We don't need to rush anything. You don't have to do anything you don't want to."

She pushes herself away from him, looks him straight in the eye, and sees his sincerity. Marianne says, "Promise you'll be here in the morning."

Seamus hesitates for a moment. "Don't worry. I'll be here when you wake up."

Marianne will never forget how safe she feels with him as they spend their first night together.

***

Their freshman year turns out to be the best of their respective lives. (*Sooner or Later by The Grass Roots*) The couple spends their time skiing, biking, waterskiing, rafting, fly-fishing, boating, kayaking, hiking, and seeing the backcountry, fully immersed in the spirit and beauty of western Montana. They attend the Foresters' Ball, for which the forestry students convert the gymnasium into an old mining camp. In the spring, they join thousands of others for the world-renowned Aber Day Kegger, a student-run benefit for the university library held at a local rodeo grounds. Kegs of beer roll down cattle chutes. Jerry Jeff Walker, Bonnie Raitt, Jimmy Buffett, the Marshall Tucker Band, and a host of other major artists play to a solid wall of college students. With their beer guzzling working its magic, Marianne and Seamus roll down a muddy hillside and come to rest in full embrace as muddy water drips from the brow of Marianne's straw cowboy hat. Amanda and Brian eventually land next to them, soaking wet from their own muddy roll as the air fills with the sounds of the Mission Mountain Wood Band.

***

When summer comes, Amanda and Marianne bring the boys up to the Flathead house. After a full day of waterskiing and cruising around the lake, Marianne and Seamus sit alone on the Andersons' dock, kicking at the water, their eyes on the jagged line of the Mission Mountains. Dusk settles in, and the range glows purple in the sun's final rays. Seamus notices Marianne's feet go still in the water beside him and glances over to see tears on her face. Seamus looks back across the lake.

"Thinking about your family, aren't you?"

Marianne muscles a smile and a nod in a poor attempt to hide her emotions. From his own experience, Seamus knows not to try to find a way to fix things. He says, "I'm truly sorry." As Marianne nervously fumbles with her locket, it unexpectedly pops open, releasing its contents somewhere on the dock. She frantically attempts to locate the material, being careful not to cause it to drop through the slats of the dock. Meanwhile, Seamus curiously reacts, helping her search for the cryptic treasure. Just as Marianne's despair seems to reach its apex, Seamus notices a small lock of hair teetering on the edge of one of the weathered boards. He carefully pinches the delicate blonde strands between his thumb and index finger, gently presenting it to Marianne. Her panic quickly dissipates, and she motions to him to place it in the palm of her hand, then returns it to her beloved ornament around her neck. Seamus stares down at the water, knowing the magnitude of the incident.

Marianne relaxes against him, knowing she's found someone she fully trusts. She again plays with the locket around her neck.

"A present from my dad," she says. "I never really told you about what happened."

Seamus pulls his feet out of the water and turns to face her. Marianne keeps her eyes on the mountains as she begins her story.

She was 13, just beginning eighth grade, when they died.

Seamus listens. When Marianne trails off, he stays quiet. Finally, he says, "What happened after the accident? You didn't move to Missoula until much later, right?"

"I don't remember too much right after, to be honest. I went to live with my grandmother, and she took care of me." Marianne pulls her gaze back from the mountains and looks squarely at Seamus. "I wish you could have met Esther. She was so beautiful. She had this power to her. This ability—and strength—to feel life in such a deep way. Sort of a gift and a curse, I guess."

"Like you," Seamus says.

Marianne gives a little half smile. "I wish. She was formidable. She was a chief's daughter. She was magical."

Marianne resumes her story. After the accident, Esther filled their days with countless hours of walking, talking, cooking, and gardening, focusing Marianne on life's simple pleasures. Every Saturday morning, they shared a hike up the canyon behind the cottage, where they would stand in the dappled sunlight beneath a giant ponderosa pine Esther called her wishing tree. Marianne's most vivid memories of the years following the accident are of helping Esther fill her window boxes and garden beds with flowers as vibrant as her grandmother's personality: lobelia, lavender, gaillardia, macedonia, and million bells.

Periodically, Marianne would watch as Esther ventured out to her manicured garden, digging up an old tin box. It was buried next to the post at the far edge of the garden, closest to the mountains. Esther would sit for a few minutes, carefully sifting through the worn container's contents. On some visits, she would add to the cache. Marianne was naturally curious about the weathered box, however she never considered digging it up, respecting her grandmother's secret.

As Esther continues to carefully monitor Marianne's emotional and spiritual state, she followed her intuition, purchasing two plane tickets to Seattle for a girls' weekend. When Esther was a younger woman, she traveled frequently with Marianne's grandfather, a tribal elder and dairy farmer, as he attended to periodic business outside the confines of Montana. After driving to Missoula, Esther and Marianne excitedly board a small airline plane destined for the Emerald City, an hour and a half flight. Upon arrival and after retrieving their luggage, Esther flagged a cab as if she had lived in the Big Apple her entire life. The taxi took them downtown, where they checked into a high-end hotel across from the beautiful city's most notable department stores and art galleries. Marianne was mesmerized and delighted, fully distracted from her tragic family memories. The two humble Montanans shopped, toured Pike Place Market, explored numerous art galleries, strolled along the water front and fed the seagulls, took in a play, and enjoyed fresh seafood. Esther successfully opens Marianne's eyes to the outside world, and with her demons temporarily at bay, Marianne had discovered a new sense of calm. As they boarded their return flight, Marianne knew she'd be back someday.

Back in Montana, the persistent nightmares returned and worsened over the course of the winter. Marianne would wake herself with her screams, reliving the accident. Esther would hold her and sing her back to sleep, and then the next night, the whole thing would start again. Esther taught Marianne how to make a dream catcher from a small hoop of willow woven with a web. They decorated it with feathers, beads, and bits of everyday life, and hung it above Marianne's bed. Esther told her the night was filled with dreams both good and bad, and the dream catcher would catch them all as they flowed by. The good dreams knew how to pass through the net's outer holes and slide down the soft feathers so gently that, many times, the sleeper did not even know he or she was dreaming. The bad dreams, not knowing the way, got tangled in the dream catcher and perished with the first light of a new day. Marianne treasured her dream catcher, but the nightmares continued.

On a wet spring morning, after a month of escalating dreams, Esther took a walk to the wishing tree alone. Marianne watched her go through the rain-streaked window and then settled back under the covers, exhausted after another harrowing night. Sometime later, half asleep, she heard her grandmother return.

Through her sleepy haze, she listened to familiar sounds from the kitchen: cupboards opening and closing, the dull crunch of the mortar and pestle, a spoon tapping on the lip of a bowl. When she finally pulled herself out of bed and opened her door, she saw her grandmother seated on the couch in the living room, far away in some type of trance. Marianne sat next to her and whispered her name, trying to hide how scared she was. Esther slowly opened her eyes and smiled. She placed her hands gently on Marianne's cheeks and said, "Another hard night, sweet girl." She was quiet for a moment, her hands still cradling Marianne's face, and then she said, "Later today, I'm going to need you to trust me."

Marianne and Esther spent the day going about their normal chores and tasks. As dusk approached, Marianne came in from the garden to find her grandmother wearing a traditional Native American dress, sipping a cup of tea. Esther again asked Marianne if she trusted her. Marianne nodded, a little nervous. Esther offered Marianne a special cup of tea, a tea different from the one Esther was sipping. Marianne took a small sip. The tea tasted of honey and earth. When they were through, they loaded into the old green Ford pickup. Esther turned onto a road Marianne had never seen before, and Marianne leaned her head against the cool glass window, dizzy and disoriented. The road, clearly seldom traveled, had a carpet of grass and moss covering the ground and a canopy of Douglas fir and western larch creating a tunnel above. "I don't feel good," Marianne said. Esther reached toward her and caressed her cheek without speaking.

Eventually, they arrived at a small hut made up of slender willow withes lashed together with rawhide and covered with animal hides. Smoke billowed from the structure's center. Esther helped Marianne down from the truck. "Sweat lodge," Esther said.

Trying to make her limbs move normally, Marianne felt a kind of peaceful bewilderment. She looked up and saw a man moving toward them from his place in front of the entrance of the sweat lodge. He started to motion to the women that they weren't allowed to enter; then, recognizing Esther's status, he quickly returned to his post and pushed the animal hide from the entrance so that Esther and Marianne could duck inside.

Marianne was hit by a wave of moist heat and the smell of

herbs. Five partially clothed men stood up, clearly taken aback by the female presence. However, after recognizing the significance of their medicine woman and her fragile patient, they settled back into their previous positions. Esther and Marianne found a spot on the mat of sweetgrass, soft cedar boughs, and sage leaves covering the ground. Staring into the sacred fire, Marianne began to hallucinate. All at once, she understood that Esther's intent was to help her find spiritual cleanliness—to purify her mind, body, spirit, and heart. As the ceremony began, Marianne's demons rushed in to haunt her, but they were soon driven off by a commanding yet gentle spirit. In the darkness and the heat, she felt a sort of return to the womb and the innocence of childhood. Her mind raced as sweat rolled down her face. Her whole body was drenched. Her grandmother seemed to levitate next to her as Marianne faded into a deep trance.

She woke to sunlight falling across her bed in Esther's cottage, feeling well-rested for the first time in months. In the kitchen, Esther was making breakfast and feeding her dog table scraps, just like any other morning. Marianne embraced her grandmother. Her innocence could never be regained, but she was soothed by the knowledge that magic was all around them. In life, pain was guaranteed, but the length of suffering was optional.

Over the next three years, Esther continued to nurture Marianne, slowly rebuilding an ordinary life. She encouraged her activities at school; when Marianne made the Polson High School varsity basketball squad as a freshman, Esther was at every game. Marianne grew up as normally as could be expected.

One hot day during the summer before Marianne's junior year, Officer Adler walked into the local fast food joint where Marianne was working. Marianne greeted her parents' best man with her usual hello—John was a regular, which Marianne suspected didn't have much to do with the quality of the burgers. He'd made it a point to check in on a steady basis ever since the accident, acting as a guardian angel of sorts. But that night, Marianne immediately noticed something in his eyes. Officer Adler took his hat in his hand and said, "I'm so sorry, Marianne." Esther had passed away earlier that day, quietly and quickly in her garden, from a pulmonary aneurism.

Seamus puts his hand on Marianne's. "I had no idea," he says. "Did the Andersons come get you after that?"

Marianne shakes her head. "They were away that summer, and they didn't even know Esther was gone. I went into foster care. Officer Adler was pretty recently divorced, so even though he tried to take me in, it wasn't going to happen. Single guy and teenage girl—not a chance.

"Anyway, the mom and the son were OK, but the father was a real chauvinist. Right wing, incredibly strict, fundamentalist. Every night at dinner, he'd display the Bible and then do a reading and then prayers."

"Oh man," Seamus says. "I can only imagine that after coming from your grandma's house—"

"I felt like I was drowning. Or suffocating. The son couldn't stand it either. But one night, we were allowed to go to this party some family friends were throwing for their sons, who were both home from college. I didn't care about the party, but I couldn't wait to get out the door. As soon as we were in the car, the son pulled a bottle of rotgut wine from under his seat. I said no—you should have smelled this stuff—and then we picked up his girlfriend and headed to the party.

"Of course, I didn't know anyone. He was ahead of me in school, and most of the other kids there were seniors or had graduated already. Anyway, to make a long story short, he introduced me to this senior, a popular kid I recognized. He played a ton of sports, and he came from one of those so-called upstanding families. We got to talking, he invited me for a ride, and we went up to the Kerr Dam reservoir. I was so glad to have someone just to talk to. But he obviously wanted something else, and he moved really, really fast. I was OK at first. It was kind of exciting. But then I wasn't, and I told him to stop. And he didn't.

"It was over really fast. He zipped up and drove me back to the party. He acted like we were on a date—put his arm around me and everything. And I didn't know what else to do, so I just stood there with him.

"When the son and I got home that night, the father was up waiting. I didn't even know we'd missed curfew. The dad got very quiet, and he leaned in and sniffed out the liquor on the kid. His voice was so even and controlled—he told him he was a disgusting sinner, and then he slapped him in the face. He sent him to bed like a child. The whole time, the only thing I wanted was to go upstairs and take a shower. But before I got up to leave, the father sat next to me, asking me questions about the night and offering his unauthentic concern for my safety. Before I knew it, he inappropriately touched my hair and creepily put his hand on my thigh. As I recoiled, he became incensed, seemingly offended by my reaction, while clearly aware of his intent. In the shadows, his wife was peering from the kitchen. I ran to my room, closed the bedroom door, praying he would not follow me. Unfortunately, the doorknob didn't lock. Fortunately, he never entered.

"I was so ashamed of myself. I couldn't stop thinking about what had happened. I hadn't even fought back at the dam. And I imagined the next weeks in that house—the next months, the next years. I couldn't stand it. After watching the doorknob for any kind of movement for a couple of hours, I packed everything I could carry, and I snuck out. I had a little money saved up from my job."

Marianne pauses and looks down, collecting her thoughts. She had never shared her story with anyone. Lifting her head, she peers into Seamus's eyes, attempting to ascertain his initial reaction. In those eyes, all she perceives is caring, no startled dread or judgment, just gentle kindness. She again looks down before looking across the massive lake, choosing to share the rest of her story.

It was raining the night she fled the foster home, a chilly rain. She hadn't given a thought to where she'd go, but a magical and magnetic homing beacon steered her back to Esther's enchanted cottage. It was three miles away, and she ran the whole way. She knew the home had been rented to another family as the estate worked its way through probate, however it seemed like her only refuge. Something drew her to the garden, and to the fencepost closet to the mountains. She dropped her backpack and began digging in the rich, muddy dirt as if a dog desperately retrieving a bone. With periodic glances toward the cottage, she finally reached the treasure. Marianne wiped the muck from its exterior before tucking it into her backpack. Again, she ran, running until she was exhausted under a Polson street lamp.

Marianne gently opened the simple box, not knowing what

to expect, but somehow knowing this was Esther's safety valve plan all along, and questioning herself why she hadn't retrieved it earlier. Inside, she discovers dried herbs and flowers between pieces of onion paper, probably rare ingredients for some of Esther's exotic potions. She discovers a small leather bag with collectible silver and gold coins and an empty weathered locket. Beneath the earthly items and collectibles, she finds various aged envelopes with postmarks dating back to the '30s and '40s. As she comes to the last envelope, she discovers a packet filled with cash, mostly $20 and $100 bills. Not a fortune, but enough to sustain during an emergency. Lastly, as she looks at the very bottom of the box, she picks out a postcard from Seattle, a card they had mailed to themselves during their trip. A wave of escapism envelops her. She repacked her backpack and headed toward Highway 93. It didn't take her long to hitch a ride as one of the men from the sweathouse drove by, heading to work in Missoula. Once they got to Missoula, he adhered to her wishes without question, dropping her off at the bus station where she quickly purchased a ticket to Seattle. On the bus, she finally sleeps, not waking until the bus travels over Snoqualmie Pass.

When she arrived at the downtown bus station, she found her way to the upscale hotel she had inhabited earlier. When the price was shared, she gasped. She methodically thanked the front desk attendee, gathering her backpack, knowing she needed to conserve her cash. After exploring her options for several hours, she eventually found a fleabag motel where she paid for several nights upfront. Scared, ashamed, and alone, she safely fell asleep as her life as a 16-year-old runaway began. (*Someone to Lay Down Beside Me by Linda Ronstadt*)

The next day, she ventured back to Pike Place Market where she secured mundane cleaning jobs at a coffee shop and at a bistro, hoping to eventually put her Polson restaurant skills to work. Inevitably, her funds begin to dwindle. At the time, she felt fortunate to identify an uninterested and independent co-worker looking to share the rent. Her cubbyhole in the undersized apartment was enough.

Six weeks into Marianne's stay, her Kerr Dam experience came back for an unexpected visit. Her mornings becoming a challenge as morning sickness commenced. It annoyed her unsympathetic roommate, but the rent money Marianne paid was worth the inconvenience. As Marianne continued to work and she began to show, a compassionate man in his 70s emerged, becoming a regular customer at the coffee shop, stopping in everyday to check on her well-being. His kindness and authentic interest resonated with her and she looked forward to his daily visits. As they become more acquainted, he was careful not to pry too deeply. She could tell he was genuinely concerned about her physical and mental well-being. He arranged periodic medical appointments for her at a mission he managed for the homeless. His name was Reverend Forman, a successful retired business man with a grown family who was called to serve the inner-city poor through the Operation Nightwatch organization. He was sympathetic, sincere, and resourceful. He kept a watchful eye on her recognizing the quality of her fragile inner spirit. A patron angel. After numerous discussions about her conflicting feelings, Marianne agreed to have the baby adopted, which Reverend Forman arranged.

Marianne delivered the baby girl a month prematurely. Literally minutes after the birth, her nurses are momentarily distracted, leaving Marianne alone with the child. Marianne took the opportunity to grab a pair of medical scissors, quickly and carefully snipping a small lock of hair from the infant. She then tucked the blonde strands under the sheets and returned the medical instrument to its rightful place. As the nurses reentered the room, they quickly recognized their error, reassessing the situation to assure Marianne and the baby's well-being. As they took the baby away, Marianne was naturally deeply conflicted. Tears flowed as she delicately placed the lock of golden hair in the locket left by Esther. She was moved into a semi-private room where Reverend Forman was seated. He hugged her as she softly sobbed.

Days after leaving the hospital, Marianne's world quickly turned chaotic as she struggled with postpartum depression. She started to miss her shifts, and more importantly, missed her rent payment to her roommate, who quickly kicked her out on the street. Desperately trying to find her bearings, Marianne approached Reverend Forman, who found temporary refuge for her at the mission. He recognized her crisis state, working diligently to find a solution.

One evening at the mission, Reverend Forman is not at dinner, and Marianne is befriended by a man in his early 20s who encourages her to venture out with him to have some fun. On the north of end of the market where many homeless reside, they share a bottle of wine until she becomes comfortably numb, laughing and enjoying his company. The young man, obviously with ulterior motives, got her to a state where she was fully vulnerable. He then reached into his pack, retrieving a syringe and needle, ready to administer the drug to his unknowing victim. Marianne was easy prey. As he commences his final procedure and begins piercing her skin, a hand seizes his wrist and the hypodermic needle skids across the worn concrete, removed before dispensing. He looks up to see a panicked Reverend Forman with a furious and aggressive Dr. Anderson behind him.

"Not on our watch," the Reverend barks, tossing the man's backpack aside as Dr. Anderson quickly ascertains her condition. The Montana doctor picked her up as Reverend Forman doubled as reconnaissance and reinforcement. After nearly a year of Dr. Anderson urgently searching the extended medical community for any trace of Marianne, her maternity stay had alerted a medical school friend who started the precise and systematic recovery. Marianne was finally safe and headed home to Montana.

"Dr. Anderson's the only one who knows," Marianne says, dropping her eyes. "Aside from you. He and Mrs. Anderson went to the courts. It was a fight—they even got Brian's dad involved, a real big-shot lawyer—and they became my legal guardians."

The light is nearly gone from the sky, and the stars have come out overhead. Only the faintest red smudge remains on the horizon. Seamus reaches out to touch Marianne's locket, and she covers his hand with her own. She rests her head on his shoulder, and they stay like that, together on the dock.

Van Blakely

Chapter 8

Later in the summer, they are able to spend some time in Seamus's neck of the woods, focusing their time in the Pintler Mountain Range and the Big Hole Valley near Wise River, close to Wisdom and Jackson. Seamus works on a ranch again, cutting hay and bucking bales, and runs, keeping in great shape. With this type of work, he barely needs to train for the upcoming football season. As Seamus shows Marianne the vast and lush valley, he shares with her his love of flying, his passion to become a pilot, and his dream of one day flying like a hawk over the Big Hole Valley. They share many hopes and dreams throughout the summer.

Marianne heads to Butte one weekend to meet Paddy, who is his usual self. Paddy is happy for his grandson and likes Marianne's spunk and adaptability. Seamus gives Marianne a tour of his and Paddy's house. Marianne looks around, absorbing the details of where Seamus grew up. In his room, Marianne jokes about the "nice picture of the Wilson sisters" on the wall. Her eyes land on a framed picture of an eight-year-old Seamus hugging his mother. She takes it in without comment. As she continues around his room, she finds the sparkling piece of quartz from the mine. She picks it up and turns it in the light.

"Where is this from?" she says.

"Oh, that's just a piece of quartz I found in the mine one day," he says. "Worthless but pretty."

Marianne studies it. As she turns it, it throws prismatic rainbows against the wall. "It's beautiful," she says. "Look how brilliant. It's like a big diamond."

"They grow like that—nature just creates that crystal look. A diamond must be cut. Sure wish it was a big diamond, though." He waits a beat and then casually says, "You can have it if you'd like."

Marianne smiles and continues her inspection before tucking it in her purse. Rummaging around in the bag, she retrieves a surprise gift for Seamus: a small dream catcher she made from material she found while in the Big Hole Valley. She describes its significance and magic, sharing the instructions Esther passed on to her. He looks into Marianne's eyes, moved.

***

A visiting football player watches as a football tumbles toward him. (*Don't Bring Me Down by the Electric Light Orchestra*) His teammates gather in front of him as they prepare for the violent onslaught. The player catches the ball, following his larger blockers. After sprinting four or five strides, the kick returner meets his doom. A colossal collision rocks the player, and he fumbles the football. A mad scrum ensues as two sets of jerseys scramble after the seemingly animate object shooting across the field. The player moans, trying to catch his breath. He looks up into his opponent's helmet, having just made close acquaintance with Mr. Seamus McElroy, who looks down and says, "It's much better to give than receive."

Seamus is playing special teams and is a second-string linebacker coming off the bench. He plays as if his hair is on fire, with the passion and athleticism of a seasoned veteran. He hustles to the sideline after forcing the fumble, blood squirting out the bridge of his nose. The trainers rush to attend to his injury; he's broken his nose. "Son of a bitch, that hurt," he says, the adrenaline waning. His coaches, trainers, and teammates congratulate Seamus with glee. After the hit by the human train, the unsuspecting victim must be redirected by several teammates as he stumbles back to his sideline. Seamus slides his helmet back on, anxious in his intensity and desire to get back on the field, regardless of his nose. The coach asks if he's all right. Seamus says, "I'm locked and loaded, Coach."

In the stands, Amanda, Brian, and Marianne cheer, passing a nip of peppermint schnapps back and forth.

***

As the fall semester gets going, Marianne half-heartedly agrees to move into her sorority house with Amanda and is busy with rush and various other Greek activities. Marianne joins a coed football team and discovers that Andrew is on the team, also. He zeroes in on her and they develop a low-key, joking friendship. Andrew is popular on campus. He's smart and socially easy, happy to spend his money taking his friends out after a scrimmage or a party. He's handsome and athletic, if not an actual athlete: he plays tennis and downhill skis, and he goes out for every intramural. When it comes to girls, he's a well-known player, but no matter who he's dating, he keeps his eye on Marianne. Andrew is unlike any of the Montana kids Marianne grew up with. He wears penny loafers, oxford shirts with the collars turned up, and khaki pants. Amanda calls him Prince Nordstrom behind his back, but Marianne thinks he looks sophisticated. Still, wary of his association with her attempted rapist, she proceeds cautiously.

***

Several games into the season, Seamus makes the travel squad. On a trip to the University of Idaho in Moscow, the whole team is tense: a couple of pro scouts are in the stands to watch three Vandal seniors. The senior linebacker playing ahead of Seamus on the depth chart goes down injured at the beginning of the fourth quarter. Seamus takes the field, and the Vandals immediately go after the freshman newcomer. But this is no ordinary freshman—Seamus is more than up for the challenge. The high-powered Idaho running game is stopped, largely by Seamus's solid play. He completely negates Idaho's senior running back, one of the pro prospects the scouts are there to see. The Grizzly announcers go crazy on the radio, saying, "Butte America can stand tall tonight." One of the scouts approaches Seamus after the game and tells him he played one hell of a game. Seamus is elated. His football career has begun.

Meanwhile, Marianne runs into Andrew at a Greek function. (*Born to Run* by Bruce Springsteen) Amanda and Brian come a bit later and notice the two of them chatting in a corner.

"What's going on with that?" Brian says.

"Oh, Prince Nordstrom? They're just friends."

"I'm not saying anything about Marianne—you know that. But that guy is a sleaze ball. You should warn her."

"Oh, come on. He's just a spoiled pretty boy; he's not that bad. Besides, I bet Marianne's a good influence on him. She doesn't give two shits how rich he is."

"He's a charming snake. You should hear the way he talks when it's only guys—he'll say he's going after 'girls with braided butt hair.'

He and his friends have this disgusting game called hogger, where they—"

"I don't want to hear what the Greek rumor mill has to say about him. Marianne likes him. I'll do my judging myself."

They're quiet for a second, watching Andrew making Marianne laugh. Then the radio behind the bar crackles, and Seamus's name comes through. Amanda leans forward and yells to the bartender, "Hey, turn it up!" She and Brian huddle as close as they can to the speaker and listen to the incredible game unfold in Idaho.

Andrew brings Marianne another beer and asks her to dance. He's on his best behavior—it's easy for him when he's with her. Amanda isn't wrong about him: he really likes Marianne, and he's doing his best to be whoever she thinks he is, and not what he fears she may suspect him of being. It seems to be working; she's friendly with him but clearly uninterested in anything else. Andrew is used to getting his way with girls, and on one level, he's intrigued by the challenge. But there's something deeper that attracts him. He likes that she's not mesmerized by his flash and will make fun of his shoes. He could never articulate it, but he has the sense that being with her would be something worthwhile.

***

Friday night of homecoming weekend arrives the following week. Homecoming hasn't changed much over the years: singing on the steps of main hall, the introduction of distinguished alumni and players, and a great Saturday morning parade. It's all pretty Norman Rockwell.

Andrew is a homecoming candidate and spots Marianne in the crowd at a pep rally. Andrew is well-oiled up by that point, but he puts on his best face as he picks his way over to meet her. She's with Amanda and some other sorority sisters, and she treats Andrew as a friendly acquaintance. Amanda watches him closely as he takes off with his friends; Brian's warning echoes in her mind. She's starting to suspect ulterior motives.

This year's homecoming game is against the Grizzlies' archrival, Montana State, the toughest and dirtiest team in the league. Seamus is slated to start the game at outside linebacker. He plays flawlessly the first quarter. Seamus is feeling his oats, knowing he is on a roll. His teammates encourage him. The Montana State coach is frustrated with his team's lack of advancement, as is the senior All-American tight end Seamus is responsible for covering. Seamus wrangles with the linemen and running backs. Paddy and his crony Frankie are behind the visitors' bench, heckling the MSU Bobcats. One of the Bobcat players takes the bait, opening with several colorful comments from the Butte contingent. Frankie ends up throwing his gin and tonic on the player as he walks away. Paddy and Frankie share a laugh as the player slides on his helmet and runs out onto the field with a slice of lime clinging to his shoulder pad.

The MSU tight end has an established reputation: big, mean, and dirty. He's already been reprimanded by the referee on several occasions. After being criticized by his coach for the third time for getting outplayed by a redshirt freshman, the player finally takes a different angle, eyeing the young linebacker. Seamus picks up another assignment, switching with the cornerback. As Seamus prepares to fill a hole in the line, the tight end illegally cracks back on Seamus's fully exposed body. The coaches and players on the sideline view the incident as if in slow motion. They try to warn him, but it's too late. Seamus doesn't see it coming. He bends grotesquely and crumples to the ground. The running back shuffles to his side and is met by Seamus's teammates, with the entire pile of humanity landing on Seamus. The pile eventually dissipates, leaving Seamus on the ground in incredible pain. Seamus tries to get up but is unable to move. Players from both teams motion to the sidelines, and the trainers arrive quickly. It doesn't take long before they call for the orthopedic doctor, who jogs out onto the field. He checks Seamus's right side. The doctor keeps his voice calm and reassuring as he explains to Seamus that he has a dislocated hip and needs to be immediately transported. The doctor motions for the EMTs to bring the ambulance onto the field.

The U of M bench is uncontrollably angry. The MSU tight end's been ejected from the game. He smiles and flips off the booing crowd as he saunters to the opposite sideline, and the crowd gets even louder. Looking at the trainers, doctors, and coaches around him, Seamus can tell he might be in real trouble. He listens to the ambulance doors slam, and the sirens start up. In his mind, he traces the ambulance's route out of the stadium. His football career is in jeopardy. He knows it. He feels it.

***

Marianne, Amanda, and Brian make it to the hospital before Seamus goes into emergency surgery. Seamus is semiconscious and visibly upset even while sedated. Marianne takes his hand. Brian stands by silently, ready to get whatever he might need. Even Amanda is quiet for once. Paddy and his closest Butte buddies rush through the hospital doors, still sporting their Grizzly attire. Paddy is worried about his grandson, not the player. When the nurse informs Paddy that Seamus is about to go into emergency surgery, Paddy is shaken. He pulls himself together for a moment, and turning so the nurse won't hear, he puts a hand on his buddy Frankie's shoulder. "You make sure MSU knows not to fuck with anyone from Butte again," he says. Frankie nods and gathers the rest of the Butte crew together.

Paddy heads into the room where Seamus is waiting. The team surgeon arrives, and as much as they want to stay, Brian, Amanda, and Marianne take their leave, going to pace the waiting room. The team surgeon reviews the situation with Paddy; Seamus is too out of it to comprehend what's going on. The surgeon explains that the hip is a ball-and-socket joint, and the socket is deep, which prevents the hip from moving in unwanted directions. With a dislocation, the patient is often unable to move the leg, and if nerve damage has occurred, it's possible there may not be feeling in the foot or ankle. It requires significant force to pop the thighbone out of its socket and dislocate. That kind of force often means someone with this injury will have other injuries, including fractures in the pelvis and legs. Paddy takes a breath as the surgeon points to the x-rays in front of him. Seamus has fractures in his right leg and his pelvis. Paddy takes notes as the surgeon talks, and then he shakes his hand. He sits down alone to wait the next hours out.

The surgery is deemed a success. Still, only time will tell about the recovery of certain nerves, and Seamus will need extensive rehabilitation. As feared, his football career is in danger. Seamus sleeps. In the waiting room, Amanda comforts Marianne.

The next morning, Brian and his father show up at the hospital. They greet Paddy and Seamus and hand over the morning paper. The front page is covered in the fallout from the game: the MSU back bus window was blown out by a shotgun while passing through Butte on I-90, and there's a picture of the MSU tight end with a black eye. Seamus shoots Paddy a disapproving look, but Paddy just shrugs. The Montana vigilantes are still intact. Brian and his dad try to make small talk with Paddy; Seamus stares out the window. For the first time, his vulnerabilities are exposed. His walls have gone up.

Van Blakely

Chapter 9

Seamus's difficult and massive rehab begins. He is frustrated, and is terrified of permanent nerve damage, but is determined to get his injured right hip back to normal. Marianne supports his efforts, going far beyond the call of duty. She helps him collect his work from classes and drives him to his rehab appointments. She's happy to stay in with him on the weekends. Seamus leans on her at first, but they both slowly become impatient with each other's needs. They begin to bicker, and a nasty, sarcastic edge enters their relationship. Seamus starts to push her away. He doesn't know what the future will bring, and that's all he can think about. He doesn't have enough left over to give to Marianne.

Seamus gets more and more impossible as the winter closes in, and Marianne misreads his anger as anger at her, not at the circumstances. He's deeply confused, and decides he needs some time alone to figure himself out. He's too young and immature to realize that the injury has challenged his identity, and he can't see what he's risking by pushing Marianne away.

For Christmas break, Seamus heads home to Butte, where he's treated like a hero. He spends most of the break drinking and partying with his high school friends. The rest of the time, he's in the bar with Paddy, wallowing in his depression and brooding on his ambiguous options.

***

Winter quarter arrives in Missoula. Missoula is a beautiful place, except in January and February, when inversion settles in the valley and makes sure it stays gray, snowy, cold, and overcast, perfect companions for Seamus's depression. Seamus decides to move into an off-campus house that Brian is sharing with three friends, a place affectionately known as the Butt Hut.

Late one winter evening, Brian walks Seamus to the Butt Hut for the first time, giving him the rundown on his future roommates. Brice and Teddy are Montana kids from Billings and Kalispell, and

Moose is a Canadian from Calgary, Alberta. Brian and Seamus turn up the walk of a shabby little house with an assortment of worn-down chairs on the porch. Inside, they find Brice on the couch, shoveling mac and cheese right out of a saucepan. "Hey," Brian says. "So, this is Seamus."

Brice pauses with the spoon halfway to his mouth. He looks a little bewildered.

"Our new roommate. Remember?" Brian says. "Is Moose home?"

Brice nods toward the bedrooms and goes on eating. Brian and Seamus knock on Moose's door. When there's no answer, Brian enters anyway. Moose is sitting on his bed in the nude, smoking a joint, playing his bass guitar with headphones on, and sporting a stitched wound on his cheek. He smiles slowly, revealing a missing tooth, and pulls off the headphones. Moose, who plays hockey for the university club team, the Flying Mules, extends his hand to greet the amused Seamus. "Caught a puck playing in a tournament in Spokane over the weekend," he says. "Tough luck."

Brian opens a window, allowing the lingering blue smoke to disperse.

On their way out, Brian asks if Teddy is home yet.

"Think he might have had one too many shots from Mr. Jäger. He's PIA," Moose says.

"Puking in action," Brian says to Seamus.

"Got it," Seamus says. "See ya, Moose."

They find an incapacitated Teddy in the fetal position next to the bathroom toilet. Brian shakes his roommate awake. "Hey, buddy, how you feelin'?"

Teddy moans. His current best friend is the cool porcelain god he's mothered up to. He props himself up to meet Seamus and immediately complains about the dry heaves. "Help me, man. I need something in my stomach."

Brian heads to the kitchen. Seamus sits on the edge of the bathtub and watches as Teddy takes his own action. He struggles to raise his head above the toilet bowl rim and then lowers his face to the cool water and laps like a dog. When Brian comes back with a 7Up, Seamus is cracking up. Teddy, toilet water dripping from his face, sinks back to his spot next to the toilet, satisfied. Brian sits down next to Seamus, and together they lose it. Brian, it turns out, can stabilize Seamus in ways Marianne can't.

***

The semester rolls on. Seamus continues to struggle with his rehab and, more importantly, his character. Marianne becomes more involved in the sorority house. They see less and less of each other, but they're still trying. Seamus finishes up his midterms earlier than Marianne does, and they spend his last night together before he heads home to Butte for spring break. The next night, drunk in Paddy's bar with all his friends, he hooks up with an ex-girlfriend. In the morning, he wakes up and immediately regrets his decision. He spends the day wandering around the house, confused and ashamed.

Meanwhile, Marianne finally makes it through her exams and goes out celebrating. She runs into Andrew at the Top Hat, a cavernous old bar crowded with drunk and happy college kids and a live band. She sees him in the long line for drinks—he sees her, calls her up to his spot in line, and buys her a beer.

"Thanks," she says, wiping beer from her top lip. She's had a few already, and she's flushed with the excitement of a night out after a long week of exams.

"You feel like a dance?" Andrew asks. They dance until they're exhausted and then talk in the back of the bar. He is shocked to find himself telling her about his family in Seattle—the whole huge dynasty, including his mom, his overbearing father, and his three older sisters. Marianne's surprised by his openness—Andrew suddenly seems like a whole person to her, someone compelling and vulnerable under all that bravado.

"It's so loud here!" Andrew yells over the band. "Would you want to continue this back at the house?" Marianne hesitates and then agrees. One thing leads to another, and Marianne spends the night.

When Marianne wakes up the next morning, Andrew is gone, having left early to catch a flight to Mexico for his final collegiate spring break. He has scored again, but this victim is different to him. In the back of his mind, Andrew feels Marianne is a woman he could really get to know. Marianne, mortified at her predicament, sneaks out of the fraternity house. She's upset at having made mistakes on so many levels, not the least of which is being left alone in the morning—a promise Seamus never broke.

***

When Seamus returns from Butte to begin the new quarter, he and Marianne do their best to hide their respective guilt. They try to get things back to normal, but after the damage their relationship suffered that winter, there's not much of a normal to get back to. The time they spend together is strained and uncomfortable. On a cold, gray March day, after fighting through another painful afternoon of total disconnect, Marianne tells Seamus she needs some space. "If it's meant to be, it will happen," she says, expressing that classic false hope.

"Come on, Marianne," he says, not wanting to believe the situation. "This is just a little spat. We'll be fine."

"It's not just a spat, Seamus. I love you, but it has been a long five months since your injury. We both need to figure some things out."

"I know things haven't been great, but they're getting better, right? It's OK; we're gonna be fine. Don't do this."

As he pleads with her, Marianne realizes how deeply in denial he is. She walks away conflicted.

***

Seamus responds by going on a bender, his Butte roots of wit and wildness on full display, with Brian and his roommates at his side. The next day they and a handful of girls head to the Lumberjack Saloon up in the Lolo National Forest, southwest of Missoula. It's a wild spot, with a bar top made from a single enormous tree trunk, a swing hung from the rafters, and cabins outside. They dance, drink, and throw horseshoes.

After spending too much time in the bar, the group drives over Lolo Pass and eventually hikes up a mile-long trail to Jerry Johnson Hot Springs, a natural, undeveloped hot springs in the Selway Wilderness.

Steam floats over a tranquil pool of water. Two bare-chested coeds relax in the hot pool with a cowboy hat floating next to them. The hat slowly rises out of the water with a smiling Seamus reappearing beneath it to the enjoyment of his companions. Brice and Moose fill their plastic cups from the half-empty pony keg sitting next to the natural pool and then quickly return to their own hot tub mates.

After a week of intense partying, Brian can't keep up with Seamus and goes home for some of his mother's cooking. Over dinner, Mr. Callaghan asks about Seamus and his hip.

"The prognosis is pretty good, actually," Brian says, "but I'm kind of worried about him. He just had his heart broken, and he's on a major bender. I don't really know what to do."

"There's not much you can do—he's got to deal with this in his own way. You know, they say there are five steps of grieving: denial, anger, bargaining, depression, and acceptance. The best thing you can do for your friend is to be consistent and stable. Seamus will be fine—his foundation is too strong. He'll work it out."

Brian listens as his dad continues.

"No matter what happens, you're both quality people going through growing pains. Unfortunately, many people have shitty things happen to them in college, and it's just a matter of how people survive it."

Brian nods, appreciating his father's advice.

When Brian returns to his house, he finds his roommates conducting a session of Bongress, with Moose, the crazy Canadian, acting as the Speaker of the House.

"A friend with weed is a friend indeed. This is our solemn creed," Moose says before taking a hit. The TV blares with a new station, MTV.

"Where's Seamus?" Brian asks.

(*Get a Haircut by George Thorogood*)

A pair of socks wiggle from under a blanket in the beanbag chair, and Seamus emerges with a crooked smile. After some banter back and forth, the doorbell rings: it's a Domino's Pizza deliveryman. Brian chuckles and digs into his wallet to cover his roommates' debt.

As he shuts the door and walks back to the halls of Bongress, the young men jump at the welcome entrance of the highly desired provisions. They thank him profusely and then sit down to veg in front of the maverick music video channel. A new Irish band named U2 appears on the screen, with a lead singer named Bono. Moose, not paying perfect attention, says, "Hey, is he really named Bongo?"

Brice momentarily chokes on a piece of pizza as Teddy blows his Rainier beer through his nose—neither can contain their laughter. "You stupid fuckin' Canadian, it's Bono."

The group shares a long laugh at the expense of Moose, who is proud of his wit.

"I'm getting really tired of these European one-hit wonders," Brice says.

Seamus just smiles and eats his pizza as Brian cracks open a beer, shaking his head.

***

Dr. Wells reviews an x-ray, trying to determine the extent of an arm break of a belligerent college student. The young man is pretty well hopped up, and Marianne's patience is beginning to wane. The police bring in another young man from the other side of the confrontation, accompanied by several of his friends. All of a sudden, a fight ensues. Dr. Wells is thrown to the floor as the police and hospital security attempt to corral the explosive situation. As the cops and orderlies restrain both sides, Dr. Wells remains out of view. The security personnel finally muscle the broken-armed man onto a gurney, although he continues to kick and throw punches. As the struggle continues, two hands holding two syringed needles strike the thighs of the patient. The patient yells in agony as the needles dig deep into his flesh. Dr. Wells slowly stands, brushing back her black hair. Marianne begins to attend to his injuries as the sedative quickly takes effect. She comments to the cops, "Looks like amateur night again."

"You've got that right, Doc."

While the broken-armed patient again yells at his bloodied adversary, Marianne leans down and whispers in his ear, "Listen, you little shit. This can go very well for you, or I can make your life miserable. What's it going to be?"

The inebriated man looks up at the doctor, studying her resolve momentarily, and then turns away to allow Marianne to do her job. After she is done casting the arm, she walks by the police officers and mutters, "Peckerheads." The cops chuckle, having done similar business with Dr. Wells on previous occasions.

Just as the commotion seems to dissipate, a 60-year-old woman is wheeled in by the EMTs. Unfortunately, Marianne recognizes this situation. The EMTs explain her plight, having bagged her since they left her home. Marianne looks out into the entryway as family and friends gather in support of the distressed and shaken husband. Marianne tries in vain to get any physical response out of the victim, but the woman is long gone, having suffered a pulmonary aneurism. Marianne notes the time to the nurse and sighs as she gathers her courage to tell the woman's family. Marianne walks into the waiting room and takes a seat next to the husband, who waits with hopeful eyes. His eyes soon fill with tears while the modern-day medicine woman's mind wanders to memories of her magical grandmother, the other medicine woman. Marianne's bizarre week continues.

***

Brian is bellied up to the bar, watching the crowd go by and munching on a hot-pepper cheeseburger. Seamus returns from the bathroom, sporting a soiled and frayed baseball cap and cowboy boots. "What took so long?" Brian says.

Seamus shakes his head. "Had to shake hands with the governor. Damn, hate to pee too early in the evening. Try to hold that first one as long as possible."

Brian nods in agreement. Two attractive girls walk by and sit down at the end of the bar, and Seamus makes a comment about one of the young ladies and her boyfriend, BOB. Brian asks who or what BOB is. Seamus, with a gleam in his eye, says, "Big ole butt."

Brian shakes his head and takes a pull of his Rainier longneck. Paddy's grandson is definitely in the house tonight.

After their "healthy" dinner, the boys decide to switch venues and walk through the downtown area to another bar.

Seamus's sobriety is on the wane. After they sit, Seamus motions with his eyes toward two cute coeds across the bar. The two girls periodically look over at Seamus and Brian. Seamus finally tips his bottle and goes back to talking with Brian. When Seamus again looks in their direction, one of the girls has lit a cigarette. Seamus is disgusted. "Christ, it's a damned shame when good-lookin' girls smoke cigarettes. Girls who put cigarettes in their mouths will put anything in their mouths."

Brian laughs, and they continue to talk. Seamus glances at the girls several times, continuing to ruminate over the cigarette. The two girls are approached by a couple of friends and are momentarily distracted. The girl sets her cigarette in the ashtray, turns toward the friend, and gives her a hug. Seamus, in his drunken state, somehow centers himself and, with the trajectory precision of a digitally programmed missile, lobs a loogie onto the now smoldering cigarette 15 feet across the bar. Brian cringes, shading his eyes as he turns away in embarrassment. Seamus innocently takes a swig of his beer as the girl eventually turns back and picks up the soggy object, disgusted. Brian hides his face, not believing what he just witnessed—it looks as if it might be a long night.

Later in the evening, Seamus sees a young lady he has shown interest in before. She's at the bar, ordering drinks for herself and her girlfriends, who are seated at a nearby table. "She definitely passes the 501 test," Seamus says. "There's something about a Montana girl in cowboy boots and 501s—damn."

"Best of luck to you," Brian says, tipping his beer.

Seamus works his way across the bar and starts a conversation.

"Hey, Seamus," the girl says.

They make small talk until Seamus asks to examine her nice new cowboy boots. Giving him a curious look, she begins to lift her foot to show him, but he shakes his head. "Take the boot off."

"Oh, come on," she says. "You can't be serious." She giggles nervously and then obliges.

Seamus hands the boot to the bartender. "Fill 'er up," he says.

The young lady tries to grab the boot back and then settles into the charade with amazement as the bartender pulls the tap. He hands the boot to Seamus, who proceeds to guzzle the beer. The girl watches in disbelief, not knowing whether to be grossed out, offended, or impressed. Seamus finishes the beer, wipes his mouth, hands her the boot, and asks her to dance to break in the new boot. The young lady rolls her eyes, slips the wet boot back on, and agrees.

Amanda and several friends come in, looking for her drunk boyfriend. Amanda greets her halfway-in-the-bag boyfriend in the appropriate fashion and then asks where Seamus is. Brian points his beer bottle toward the dance floor, where the now-hammered Seamus is slow dancing to a smutty song (*Just Between You and Me by April Wine*) and draping himself over his willing prey with a satisfied grin on his face. "Christ Almighty, Brian, some friend you are," Amanda says, shaking her head. Brian just smiles and shrugs.

After the music stops, the young lady goes to the restroom, and Seamus returns to his friends. Seamus gives Amanda a long, drunken hug, much to her chagrin. Amanda makes a snide comment about Seamus's behavior, maternally giving him crap about his current state. However, wit is best fought with wit. He responds, "It's better to burn out than fade away," attempting to startle the unflappable Amanda. Amanda shakes her head, half disgusted and half entertained.

She contemplates for a moment before removing her jacket and exposing her shapely figure under a tight sweater and 501s. With a sexy look over her shoulder, she saunters over to the jukebox, drops in a coin, and then purposely and seductively bends over to choose a song. A raunchy rock song begins to play. (*I Hate Myself for Loving You by Joan Jett*) She strolls toward Seamus and grabs him by a belt loop, saying, "It's time to test that hip."

Amanda begins to dirty dance, grinding on Seamus. Seamus tries to dance, but is taken aback by her aggressiveness. He looks back to Brian, who is now laughing hysterically as Seamus attempts to dance in his dumbfounded and inebriated state. Seamus's previous dance partner returns from the restroom and joins the two of them. Seamus enjoys dancing with two women until Amanda chooses to dance exclusively with the other woman, who obliges. Seamus, confused, has the look of a cow looking at a new gate. Halfway through the song, Amanda whispers, "Gotta run, big fella." Seamus, still stunned and humbled, staggers back to the bar with the other woman. Amanda has won this round of wits.

Amanda gives Brian a passing glance, once again revealing her spunky confidence. Seamus dazedly walks up to him and says, "You're a very lucky man, aren't you?"

Brian smiles, finishes the last ounces of his beer, and says, "Yes, I am."

Seamus grins, knowing Amanda just smoked him. Brian joins Amanda and starts to head out. As the couple reaches the doorway, Seamus shouts, "Hey, Brian, go ugly early and beat the two o'clock rush, huh?" Amanda shoots a disapproving glare back at her dance partner. Brian grins.

On their way out, Brian accidentally bumps into six fraternity boys—neither Brian nor Amanda recognize Andrew in the bunch. Brian excuses himself and Amanda, continuing out to the sidewalk. Four of the frat rats turn and follow them outside, while Andrew and another hang back to watch the action. One of the frat boys shoves Brian in the back, eager for a fight. "Hey, I said I'm sorry. I don't want any trouble," Brian says.

Amanda gets nervous and mouthy as the largest frat rat gets in Brian's space. He's a balding, pit-bull-looking guy with bad acne, no doubt on steroids, and he's out looking for trouble. "Keep your slut in line," he says.

"Go to hell, you piece of shit," Brian says. The fighter punches Brian a couple times and then stands back to watch as he falls to the ground. Amanda goes to help Brian up, not noticing Andrew in the background. Amanda then begins to give *Homo erectus* a piece of her mind, making the spectators laugh. Brian regains his senses and motions to Amanda to stay put. A crowd has now gathered around and is encouraging the bout as the more aggressive and capable opponent continues to bark down at Brian, pushing him to the ground whenever he tries to get up.

Suddenly, Brian recognizes that *Homo erectus's* glaring look has shifted over Brian's shoulder. A voice follows. "Hey, Lucky, what's goin' on? I thought you and Amanda were headed home." Seamus strolls up to his friend, momentarily leaving his newfound date, and offers his hand to help Brian up.

"You don't need to get involved here," *Homo erectus* says, taking a step back despite his swagger.

"Oh, I think I do," Seamus says, stepping into the pit bull's space.

"Who the fuck are you, anyway?"

Seamus straightens up, reviewing his surroundings, and then turns slowly to view his adversary. "Have we ever met before?"

The fighter smarts off.

Seamus references the Flintstones, saying, "I'm Barney Rubble's older brother, Tee T-Rubble."

The gathered crowd laughs. *Homo erectus*, not getting the play on words at first, continues to mouth off.

Seamus smiles, nosing up to the muscle-head. "I'd like you to do me a favor. It's now time for you to give your soul to Jesus, because your ass is mine, you miserable piece of shit. By the way, I like the sound you make when you shut the fuck up."

Homo erectus, unfortunately for him, takes the first swing at the Mining City bar rat. The poor young man has no idea what kind of fury he has just unleashed. Seamus shows his power and Butte bar upbringing, quickly taking out *Homo erectus* and three others with some help from Brian.

Seamus stares into the crowd and turns away, not willing to stoop any lower. The throng begins to disperse, and Seamus turns to check on Brian. He brushes him off and makes light of the situation. Amanda marvels at Seamus's strength, loyalty, and heart. Brice, Teddy, and Moose finally show up after the festivities have subsided—they heard about the goings-on while at a bar down the street. Moose showboats as if he could have actually done anything. Seamus, checking a bleeding knuckle, jokes with Moose about his fighting abilities without a hockey stick.

Amanda underestimated his and Brian's friendship—she had no idea Seamus had this side and is touched by his devotion. Seamus winks at his friends, downplaying the event. "I feel like I'm back in Butte," he says. He puts his arm around his lady friend and walks away nonchalantly with a Rainier beer bottle in his hand. As he walks away he flashes a hang-ten sign. Amanda, Brian, and the roommates look on with admiration.

***

The following Sunday morning, Seamus receives a call. He walks to the phone in his boxers, scratching himself. Unshaven and with hair sticking out everywhere, he is dealing with a nasty hangover. Brice hands him the phone while Moose pours himself a bowl of Cap'n Crunch with chocolate milk. It's Paddy's friend Frankie. Paddy has had a stroke and is incapacitated. Seamus listens intently, sobering up immediately. Sensing a problem, Brice wakes Brian. Seamus tells his roommates an abbreviated version of the situation and hurriedly packs his bags. He leaves for Butte as quickly as possible.

When Seamus arrives at the Butte hospital, Paddy is in bad shape. He barely recognizes Seamus and is paralyzed on his left side. The doctors tell Seamus that while Paddy will eventually be able to leave the hospital, he'll require constant care. Seamus calls Brian and asks him to withdraw him from classes and ship his belongings. Brian says, "Do you need help? I can drive your stuff over myself."

"Drive it or ship it—whatever is easier," Seamus says. "Thanks, though."

"Call me if you need anything," Brian says, but he knows he won't be hearing from Seamus for a while.

Seamus goes back to the mine, working extra hours in addition to running the bar and the household, doing his best to pay for Paddy's uninsured care. Fun, frolic, and dreams are no longer a priority or a reality. Seamus, once self-absorbed by his own health and future, has had his foundation rocked to the core. He's been disconnected from his comfort zone. He quickly recognizes the insignificance of his previous situation and adjusts his priorities.

Chapter 10

A radiant bride walks up the church aisle in a packed church, on the arm of a proud and smiling Dr. Anderson. He lifts the bride's veil, revealing Marianne's face. She smiles, kisses him on the cheek, and gives him a long hug. Dr. Anderson shakes the hand of the groom and offers Marianne's hand. Marianne's hopeful eyes search the eyes of her soon-to-be husband, Andrew. Amanda, the maid of honor, observes, caring but cautious. When Marianne turns and somewhat hesitantly takes her vows, her profile subtly exposes her pregnancy. A festive and raucous college reception follows. (*Paradise by the Dashboard Light by Meat Loaf*)

***

A leader and fly land on the water. After a short wait, a trout aggressively strikes the metal and thread, quickly realizing its unforgiving decision. Several months after Paddy's stroke, Brian has traveled to the McElroy ranch to fish the Big Hole River with Seamus. Brian is surprised to see Seamus sporting longer hair and hiding behind a beard. He recognizes how hard Seamus is working and how much he is hurting. Having visited Paddy earlier that day, Brian realizes the severity of the situation: Paddy doesn't have health insurance and was not the best financial manager. After getting a full-blown tour of Butte, Brian finally sees and understands where Seamus comes from, and he respects him even more.

On the river, Brian says, "So what are you thinking about college these days?" Seamus looks skeptically at his friend, and Brian lowers his head. "OK. I'll be honest—your coach, the athletic director, and some of the alumni, including my dad, wanted me to ask about your intentions. But I'm also asking as your friend."

Seamus looks out on the horizon, contemplating the obvious. "My hip is fine, and I know Paddy would want me to go back, but my heart is here with him. He's my only family. I'm starting at Montana Tech next fall." Seamus casts. "It's in Butte, and they've got a great mining engineering school and a decent business department, so I'm set. The whole football-star thing just doesn't seem as important as it used to."

The two friends fish in silence for a bit before Brian broaches the topic they're both avoiding. "So, I don't know if you heard, but Marianne got married."

"Yeah, I heard. Andrew, huh? I hope they're happy."

"You OK?" Brian says. He can see the way Seamus is shrugging it off, and he knows his true feelings.

"Relationships are all about timing and connectivity. Between the injury, my problems dealing with it, and Paddy, the stars just didn't line up." Seamus peers over the tranquil waters, considering what might have been. Brian ties a new fly on his line as Seamus continues to row them down the river.

***

After the wedding, Andrew and Marianne head to Seattle. Andrew begins working in his father's stock brokerage firm, taking advantage of his father's extensive social network of wealthy Puget Sound-based clients. (*Power of Gold by Dan Fogelberg*) He is smart, cunning, and coldly shrewd. With his father's connections and his wily, if not manipulative, nature, his career is hardwired for success, churning and burning less astute clientele. As his family's only son, Andrew has a lot of expectations riding on his shoulders; failure isn't an option. But as his redeeming qualities start to dwindle, the genesis of another American Pharisee was on full display, with Marianne a victim of his hypocrisy and hubris.

In winter, Marianne gives birth to a boy, whom she names Colin. She's smitten. She loves being a mother and is happy in her new life. Marianne and Andrew live a materialistic existence foreign to the earthier Marianne, but she feels secure and satisfied. Andrew's family is big and loud and absorbs her immediately. She gets along well with his mother and his sisters, if not his dad, and she loves the idea of raising her kids in this stable, strong family structure. She temporarily puts her schooling on the back burner.

***

Baby cereal is poured into a bowl and stirred. The television hums in the background as apple sauce and creamed corn are prepared. Seamus takes the bowl down the hallway and enters the family room, where the semi-invalid Paddy is propped up in front of the television, waiting for his dinner. As Seamus patiently begins to feed his grandfather, he looks exhausted. Working in the mine, overseeing the bar, taking care of Paddy, and taking classes at the college, he is spent. His normally sparkling eyes show little sign of hope. His dreams have deserted him.

Seamus sighs and bows his head, resting as he waits for Paddy to swallow his food. After taking several spoonfuls of food, Paddy suddenly spits up, temporarily breaking Seamus's spirit and patience. Seamus jumps up, searching the home in a rage for a dishrag. As he swears to himself and cleans up the mess, he notices a tear roll down Paddy's weathered cheek. Seamus looks into Paddy's pleading eyes, recognizing that his beloved grandfather is still with him in spirit. He regroups. Seamus hugs his grandfather as a Miami Vice banana boat roars by on the television.

***

Once more, Dr. Anderson proudly walks down the church aisle with a veiled bride on his arm. Familiar faces adorn both sides of the church. On the bridesmaid side, sorority sisters, high school cheerleaders, and the maid of honor, Marianne, beam at the bride's entrance. On the groomsmen side, Brice, Teddy, and Moose anxiously await as Brian leans over to talk with his best man, his high school friend Steve. As Dr. Anderson presents his daughter to Brian and the pastor begins the service, Marianne glances across toward Steve—she knows the real best man is not in attendance today.

At the reception, a suspender-clad Andrew is large and in charge, catching up with old acquaintances and boasting about his professional accomplishments. (*Mainstreet by Bob Seger*) Meanwhile, Marianne chases their young son, Colin, around the reception hall, doing her best to perform her wedding duties at the same time.

During a dance with Brian, Marianne asks about Seamus. Brian looks at her for a moment and then says, "He's doing fine." He's not willing to disclose the true situation; he doesn't want to mar the spirit of the day.

"Good," Marianne says. She appreciates Brian's commitment to Seamus's confidentiality.

A small person walks toward Marianne and Brian on the dance floor. Marianne reaches down to pick up Colin, whom Andrew has evidently lost track of during his socializing. Marianne wrinkles her nose—Colin has filled his diaper. Brian takes the situation in, watching as Marianne heads off to the bathroom to change him. When Marianne returns, Brian and Amanda are lost in a dance together. Marianne, holding Colin, looks intently at her two friends, a momentary twinge of sadness showing through. She's happy for her friends, but she's beginning to recognize her marital plight.

Chapter 11

A flower-covered casket lies in front of the carved wooden altar. Father Matule closes his Bible, carefully places the weathered book on the pulpit, and folds his hands. He stands, head bowed. After several reflective moments, he raises his head with a reassuring and welcoming smile. He begins his homily.

"What does it mean to be spiritually mature? Spiritual maturity understands that theology—that is, the written statement of beliefs—is important but not as important as actual daily spiritual practice. It understands that the difference between theology and actual spiritual practice is the difference between reading a menu and having dinner. This kind of maturity realizes that beliefs are internal, and our beliefs should meet our needs but never be forced on others. Spiritual maturity is flexible, meaning our way of believing is not the only way. It realizes that religious certainty can lead to closed-mindedness. As a result, spiritual maturity rejects the 'My way or the highway' approach to life. Religious certainty is the antithesis of this characteristic and can also be insulting to other faiths. Spiritual maturity understands that religious certainty can be divisive rather than inclusive and would rather talk about how we are alike than how we are different.

"Spiritual maturity is profoundly democratic; it believes all individuals are empowered to discover what is sacred and liberating for them. In doing this, it understands that strong faith is not the opposite of reason and is not infallible. It welcomes continued questioning and wondering; it doesn't mind being challenged, and it is willing to grow and change if further knowledge and insights lead to that conclusion. Spiritual maturity understands that we must learn to live with life's ambiguities and unfair turns and, for our faith to be well founded, all our prayers don't necessarily have to be answered. It understands there are difficult things in life that must be endured, and when those difficult things arrive, we need to be wise enough to understand that we may gain strength, courage, and confidence by every experience in which we really stop to look fear in the face. Spiritual maturity is what allows all of us to turn suffering into compassion.

"Spiritual maturity is patient and understands that sometimes the hard things in life require a change of attitude: a change from viewing those difficult things as burdensome obligations to instead seeing them as blessed opportunities. Its patience believes as we mature, we may develop, allowing time for reflection, added perspective, and wisdom. Yet at the same time, spiritual maturity understands that the passage of time doesn't necessarily equate to added perspective and wisdom; sometimes the young fool only grows to be the old fool."

The priest pauses to retain his composure and then gently smiles as he addresses his old friend. "My beloved childhood friend Paddy McElroy used to quote an old Scottish proverb that says, 'Adversity is the diamond dust heaven polishes its jewels with.' Spiritual maturity often morphs from adversity. It is marked by a profound and unrelenting kindness: the capacity to agonize in the troubles of others, but also to truly rejoice in the good fortune of others. Spiritual maturity speaks for itself."

The priest crosses himself and drops his head to say a short prayer. He then looks out at his congregation, taking a deep breath. He looks down, fatherly, upon a sobbing Seamus in the front pew. Father Matule is satisfied that his message was heard and understood by its intended recipient.

***

A black BMW sports car glistens on the showroom floor. The voices of Andrew and the car salesman banter back and forth as they vie for negotiating position. In the background, an uninterested Marianne holds her toddler, Colin, in one arm with her backpack over her other shoulder. Andrew is well dressed and manicured, while Marianne looks like a disheveled mother who is attempting to find time to study for an exam. Andrew eventually asks for Marianne's opinion regarding the car, and Marianne reminds him that she needs to get to the library to study for her MCATs to enter medical school. Andrew ignores her concerns, again observing the fine German automobile and finally agreeing to make the purchase. Marianne rolls her eyes, knowing the car is just supporting their excessive lifestyle. Marianne sticks around long enough to sign the finance documents and retrieves Colin before she jumps in her worn Dodge minivan, headed toward the babysitter and then to the University of Washington library.

***

At Paddy's bar several weeks later, the bookkeeper hands a drained, yet relieved, Seamus the day's mail. "Thanks for picking it up," Seamus says, heading for the door. "I'm late for an appointment."

She watches, knowing how much his life has changed, as Seamus climbs into his old truck, mail in hand.

After the old Chevy struggles to a start, Seamus makes his way through his hometown and eventually stops in a parking lot. He quickly sorts through the mail on the seat next to him, pulling a large envelope to the front of the pile. He opens it with some pride: it's his Montana Tech diploma, a bachelor's degree in mining engineering with a business minor. He continues to sort through the mail until he comes upon a thick envelope. He inspects it carefully and then places it on the dashboard and exits the vehicle.

He walks into the squat building behind the parking lot, an attorney's office, where Paddy's friend Frankie waits. Frankie stands and hugs him hard, nearly forcing the air from Seamus's lungs. After a long embrace and some brief explanations and signatures, Seamus hands Frankie the tavern's title and the key. "Don't give away too many freebies," Seamus jokes. Frankie recalls Paddy's familiar admonition, noticeably saddened by his friend's departure.

***

Forty-five-pound plates slide onto a bar, three plates per side on the bench press. (*Limelight by Rush*) Including the bar, it's 315 pounds. The now clean-shaven Seamus lies down and quietly pumps out ten reps. He works out at this dilapidated boxing club in uptown Butte with the vengeance he once displayed on the football field. He works through his pain; his tenacity and focus as apparent as his rebuilt confidence. He is finally free from the limelight. He has awoken from his nightmare.

Seamus sells Paddy's home to a high school football friend and his very pregnant wife, handing them the keys and laughing as his jubilant friend attempts to carry his wife over the threshold. He drives up the Big Hole Valley and throws sticks into the river for Angus. Seamus loves this valley. He kneels down to whisper into Angus's cropped ears, "We're going to keep the ranch." Angus voices his approval.

Back in Butte, Seamus stops at his parish with the thick envelope, sharing his plans with Father Matule and accepting some parting wisdom. Seamus comforts the priest as they share a tender moment. To finish his goodbyes, Seamus drives to the top of the Continental Divide to visit the immense Lady of the Rockies statue overlooking the Mining City. He ponders his future as he says farewell to his home. As he begins his journey eastbound on I-90 through Homestake Pass, he looks in his rearview mirror and then over at Angus, who's panting with excitement while sitting in the passenger's seat rather than his usual spot in the truck bed. On the seat between Seamus and Angus is a letter with a South Bend, Indiana, postmark. In the top left corner is the embossed address of Notre Dame's Mendoza College of Business Graduate School.

Chapter 12

A swimmer makes her way through the chilly, choppy waters of Lake Washington. Around her, a school of other swimmers head to the shore. Marianne's stroke remains strong as she attempts not to get kicked by a fellow competitor and to gauge a safe exit location. When she finds land, she makes her way up the embankment. As she exits the water, the air is filled with positive energy at the all-women Danskin Triathlon in Seattle. Shouts of encouragement and individual names come from the supportive crowd as she makes her way to the next stage of the event. However, as Marianne approaches the bike station, she hears, "Move your ass," which immediately brings a smile to her face as aghast onlookers direct their nuclear stink eye.

Marianne, without hesitation, shouts back, "Help me find my damn bike!"

As Marianne gets closer, Amanda, sporting a "Cancer Sucks" shirt and a Montana Grizzlies baseball cap, helps her find her bike location and her change of clothes, not necessarily following the rules. Bending over to help her friend, Amanda's cap falls off, revealing her bald scalp. Undeterred and defiant, she helps Marianne change her clothing and mount her bike for her impending 25-kilometer ride. As Marianne rides away, she looks back to see Amanda shouting colorful comments. Cancer, Marianne muses to herself as she turns and focuses on pedaling, chose the wrong opponent in Amanda. It didn't stand a chance. She would win this battle.

Hours later at the triathlon's finish line, Marianne is greeted by her now emotional friend with open arms, and tears flow as they share a long embrace. Amanda whispers in her ear, "Thank you."

Andrew eventually joins the two friends after getting caught up in a social discussion with an acquaintance. He gives Marianne a peck on the cheek and congratulates her on finishing the race, also commenting on all the shapes and sizes of the women running the race. Amanda does her best to bite her lip.

***

Fall 2014

Marianne and Andrew are seated in a well-furnished, impeccable waiting room—what must have once been the living room of a fine old house. Andrew checks the newspaper sitting on the glass coffee table. Marianne sits at the other end of the long sofa, her eyes on the window. Neither one speaks. Finally, the silence is broken by the sound of a door opening, and their marriage counselor appears. She ushers Andrew and Marianne back to her office and waits while they settle in. The counselor looks back and forth at them and asks, "So, what brings you here today?"

Marianne readies herself to speak—she is the one who brought them here, with Andrew kicking and screaming all the way, and she's not expecting him to step up now. Searching for the right words, she wonders whether to address his infidelity right off the bat, or whether that's too aggressive. She wonders if there's a gentler way into this, one that will give their marriage a fighting chance.

Andrew leans forward, his hands on his knees. "Well, I think I'm the one who brought us here, if I'm perfectly honest," he says. "I hate to admit it, but it's true."

Marianne recognizes the way he's sitting; his smooth, rich tone; the little truth covering up the big lie. He goes on. "I messed up big-time. My wife is an incredible woman. But we've been married a long time, and I think sometimes I lose sight of that." He shakes his head and gives a little rueful smile. "I've had a rough time with work lately—I think I've just been so focused on trying to get that back on track that I've let my marriage go right off the rails." Andrew reaches for Marianne's hand, his face expressing contriteness. The counselor nods, listening.

It's all his usual charming bullshit. Half of Marianne can't believe what she's hearing; the other half of her never expected anything else. She thinks back over the decades of their marriage. Her initial period of happiness faded as Andrew got sucked up into the family business and the cycle of making and spending money. She first started to suspect his cheating as she finished up her BA and then applied for med school at the University of Washington; she was caring for Colin and studying constantly, and whatever emotional depth or connectivity they cultivated in those early days evaporated. She settled into their cold marriage, focusing on Colin and school and stepping into the role of society wife when Andrew needed her to. Andrew focused on living up to some image in his mind of what it meant to be his father's only son. He continued to thrive financially as he rode the wave of new Puget Sound wealth.

She didn't confront him about his cheating until the middle of her residency, when she caught him red-handed in the family's downtown condo. They had moved to Bainbridge Island across Puget Sound, commuting by ferry to the city. The condo allowed her to rest between shifts, and the island setting was more in line with her earthy nature. However, it ultimately offered Andrew a location to pursue his infidelity. After the transgression, he apologized repeatedly, blamed it on numerous factors, and agreed to go to counseling. Marianne felt trapped: Andrew was paying off her school loans and paying for the nanny who made her crowded schedule possible. She wanted Colin to grow up in an undivided home and have the solid family life she'd lost so young. Devastated, she agreed to stay in the marriage. Some months after the incident, when Marianne discovered she was pregnant with Polly, she came to see that nothing had changed. For Andrew, a new baby just bought him more time.

As the years went on, Andrew came to specialize in a subtle emotional abuse. He knew Marianne's weak spots and knew how a perfectly timed comment could crush her confidence and keep her in line. He played on her fears of being an absent mother and held her debt to him over her head. Worn thin by the degradation and feeling the weight of the responsibilities of her job and her family, Marianne saw her self-esteem erode. She was aging under the strain, which Andrew never failed to note. Her thriving professional self-regard remained her foundation, but being a mom remained Marianne's top priority. She relished every second with her children. Her other cornerstone was volunteering her medical expertise at Operation Nightwatch, following in Reverend Forman's footsteps. Even though her regular medical rounds fed her professional passion, her time helping others navigate rough times seemed more rewarding, having uniquely seen both ends of the spectrum. The stark difference of providing care for Boeing, Microsoft, Starbucks and Amazon families from Redmond,

Kirkland, and Bellevue contrasted her efforts serving her less fortunate inner-city patients, keeping her grounded and reflective while allowing her to face her own lingering demons.

Andrew participated in family activities when necessary, convenient, and public. Polly turned out to be a lot like Marianne, and from the beginning, Andrew struggled to connect with her. He bonded with Colin over sports; as Colin grew up, it became clear he was an exceptional athlete. Andrew coached football and baseball, his son's talent feeding his ego. As Colin reached his late teens, however, his gentle, contemplative nature began to clash with his father's, and he became disenchanted with Andrew. Colin eventually received a full-ride football scholarship to the University of Montana, where he thrived on and off the field. He chose to study environmental studies, much to Andrew's chagrin and dismay.

By 2008, Marianne had been on the verge of leaving Andrew; her work in the ER had finally allowed her some financial independence, and she felt the kids were old enough to handle the split. Then, during the financial meltdown, Andrew got caught financially overextended on several shady and mortgage-backed investments and, worse, was peripherally linked to a highly publicized and complex scheme to defraud investors. Creative legal maneuvering and Andrew's family ties kept him at a distance from most formal charges, but he was hit with a devastating financial settlement, and his Washington brokerage license was suspended. However, his smooth demeanor and scheming confidence remained intact, taking a toll on Marianne's soul.

Marianne recommitted herself to the marriage—she wasn't going to leave him at his lowest point. She set down her simple, non-negotiable terms: The family would move back to Missoula, where she secured a position at St. Patrick's, used the family savings to buy a house, and set up their new life. She supported the family while Andrew took a few years off and then established a Missoula branch of the Wells family real estate dynasty.

Polly flourished in Missoula, growing close with Amanda and Brian's daughters and relishing the time outdoors. Meanwhile, Colin finished up his graduate work at the University of Washington. He took a position as a religious studies and philosophy professor at Seattle University, married, and presented Marianne with a grandchild she dotes on from afar. Marianne's kids are in good shape.

Andrew is still talking; the counselor is still nodding. Marianne takes her hand back from his grasp. "If Andrew insists on playing games, I would like to play a game as well," she says. "May I please have a piece of paper?"

The counselor tears a piece from the pad beside her and offers Marianne a pen.

Marianne says, "Let's play *Wheel of Fortune.*" She draws nine spaces on a piece of paper, baiting Andrew to play the game.

Andrew is nervous; she can tell. He makes a couple of guesses, reluctantly playing along. With each correct letter, Marianne praises him: "Oh, very nice, Andrew. What astute ability." After filling in a couple of consonants, Marianne cuts him off. "Dr. Wilson, I would like to buy a vowel," she says. "Dr. Wilson, I would like to buy an I." She fills in the letter. "Dr. Wilson, I would like to buy another vowel. I'd like to buy an A." She fills in the second vowel. "Dr. Wilson, I would like to solve the puzzle, because I'm done playing games." She fills in the rest of the puzzle, stands up, tosses Andrew the piece of paper, and then walks out of the office. (*Already Gone by the Eagles*)

Andrew and the counselor are stunned for a moment. Then Andrew looks down and reads the paper: "Kiss My Ass." He shakes his head and laughs a little, trying to save face with the counselor. "I'm so sorry about this," he says, gathering their things.

He follows Marianne out to the parking lot, where she's digging through her bag for the car key. "Nice to see you've still got some fire in you," he says. "You want to come back in and talk about this like adults?"

Marianne puts the key in the car door and looks over the car at Andrew, her eyes cold. In a flash, Andrew realizes that things have changed—he has officially gone over the line.

Marianne speeds out of the parking lot, flipping him off as she drives away. She has woken up.

Van Blakely

Chapter 13

It's Friday night during homecoming weekend. A festive crowd packs the Depot, a popular upscale Missoula restaurant. Amanda and Brian run into Marianne and Andrew, who are out to dinner with some of Andrew's friends. It's obvious from Marianne's remote politeness that she is simply completing an obligation.

While they socialize, Colin strolls into the restaurant, home for the weekend from Seattle. Marianne comes to life when she sees him. He gives her a long hug and then shakes his father's hand politely—their relationship is strained, at best. "Still got that hair, I see," Andrew says, nodding toward his son's ponytail. "The five-day scruff's a nice touch."

Colin shoots Marianne a look, and she rolls her eyes slightly.

Andrew doesn't notice. He rattles the ice in his glass. "About time for another scotch and soda. Anybody want one? Colin?" He moves off toward the bar.

When he returns, Colin is deep in conversation with Brian, who wants to know all about his new teaching position. Andrew drink in hand, has a big wet spot on his pants. "Some asshole bumped into me at the bar and spilled my drink all over me," he says. "Bartender took forever making a new one. What'd I miss?"

Colin goes back to filling Brian in on his current research and teaching, trying to make some room in the conversation for his dad. However, Andrew is a few drinks in and out of his depth— he's had a hard time reconciling this quiet scholar with his vision of his son as a football hero. It doesn't take long before he diverts the conversation to Colin's past glory days on the football field. Colin is disinterested in his father's antics. When he spots some college friends across the bar, he makes a quick exit.

Andrew continues to be Andrew with his friends. Brian eventually excuses himself before turning to Amanda and whispering, "What a prick."

Amanda lingers for a bit, not wanting to abandon Marianne. "You OK? You seem down tonight," she says.

"I'm fine. Tired, I guess. This whole thing just takes a lot of energy." Marianne pauses. "Homecoming is always a tough time for me for some reason."

Later in the evening, Andrew is still going strong. More college buddies have arrived, and he looks as if he's settled in for the long haul. Marianne politely excuses herself and heads to the restroom. Watching her go, one of Andrew's friend's comments on how good Marianne looks. Andrew glares across the table at his friend and says, "If it floats, flies, or fucks, it's better to rent."

When she returns, Marianne demands they head home together, or she'll get a ride from Brian and Amanda. He begrudgingly agrees to take her home, complaining to his friends about what a pain in the ass she is. Andrew has had too much to drink. He loudly weaves from the restaurant area past the adjacent bar and into the parking lot—he's back on the subject of the asshole who spilled a drink on him at the bar. As they walk toward the car, Marianne needles him about being drunk. "Give me the keys," she says. "There's no way you're driving in that state."

"What state is that, Marianne, huh? It's my car. I'm fucking driving."

Marianne bows sarcastically, and Andrew recognizes an attitude. He slaps her hard. Marianne, stunned and disoriented, holds her cheek. She can't make sense of what just happened.

In the silence afterward, Andrew recognizes his error. "I'm so sorry, baby," he says, "I'm so, so sorry. You're right—I'm drunk. I don't know what I'm doing. God, Marianne, I'm sorry." He reaches out to touch her shoulder.

"Don't you touch me," Marianne says, her voice rising. She grabs the keys from his hand. "You drunk, cowardly, cheating, lying, spineless bastard. You're not worth the air you waste. I'm driving myself home. You can find your own goddamn way." Out of the corner of her eye, she's aware of some movement in the shadows by the restaurant. She slams the car door and drives hurriedly out of the parking lot.

An unfinished bottle of Rainier beer sits unattended at the bar.

***

Homecoming weekends in Missoula are fabulous. The maples

are losing their leaves, there is a nip in the air, and people are wearing sweaters. The homecoming parade hasn't changed much since the '70s: It's still got that Norman Rockwell feeling and those all-American qualities. There are bands of all ages, floats, kids, sirens, politicians, baton twirlers, and lots of good, clean fun.

Amanda and Brian are on the sidelines, watching for their two high-school-aged daughters to go by in the parade. Andrew and Marianne arrive by themselves. Andrew is hungover, sporting sunglasses to hide from the bright sun. He quickly finds some fraternity friends and a Bloody Mary. Marianne is bundled up and standing in the background by herself. Amanda eventually spots her friend, gives her a hug, and asks what happened the night before— Andrew came back into the bar drunk and upset, looking for a ride home. Marianne chooses not to share any details, just saying she got fed up with his antics. Amanda heads back to join Brian.

The bands roll by. Polly rides on a float, waving proudly to her mother. Marianne returns the wave, smiles, and snaps a photo, happy to see her beautiful daughter. As she lowers her camera, she hears Andrew in the background and shudders. She tries to keep her focus on the parade and the crowd, chatting with other onlookers. While she talks to another mother, she recognizes someone in the crowd on the other side of the street. She does a double take, but the familiar face has disappeared. She continues to chat, but she's distracted and keeps scanning the crowd on the other side.

A few moments later, she sees a man hugging Amanda and then Brian. The hug with Brian lasts longer than she'd have expected. Marianne's curious—she can't get a good look at him, but something in the way he holds himself seems familiar. When he turns, it takes Marianne a moment to recognize him with his slight frame, but when she makes eye contact, she instantly knows: it's Seamus. She's overwhelmed, first by excitement, and then by embarrassment at her appearance and overall circumstances. She looks away. When she looks back, the trio is gone. She strains, almost in desperation, to find them in the crowd. Suddenly, she is tapped on the shoulder; she turns and, without thinking, gives Seamus a hug. Meanwhile, Andrew is wrapped up with his friends and another Bloody Mary.

Seamus looks incredible; he's tan, fit, and starting to gray at the temples. He appears at peace with himself and exudes a humble confidence. Marianne stumbles her way through some small talk—she can tell they're both avoiding more personal topics.

"It is so good to see you," she says. "As you can see, not much has changed around here." Marianne waves toward the parade.

Seamus responds, "Honestly, seeing it now, I'm sorry I didn't come back earlier. I was always worried it'd be more like Halloween than homecoming." When Marianne raises an eyebrow, he goes on. "Seems like a weekend full of rattling skeletons, frightful goblins, and haunting ghosts."

"And where do I fit in?"

Seamus grins. "I think you know, Casper."

The conversation eventually strains as they exchange more pleasantries, telling each other they hope to see each other later during the weekend. "Hope your husband recovered from that tongue-lashing he got last night. Make sure to tell him I'll cover his dry cleaning." Seamus winks, gives her another hug, and walks off with a subtle limp, favoring his left side.

Marianne stands alone for a few seconds, attempting to hold back her tears. The parade ends. Andrew yells at her to come with him. Once again, she shudders with disgust.

✳✳✳

It's halftime, which means tailgate time at the Griz football game. Marianne stands off to the side of the festivities with Amanda while the smells of barbecue, bratwurst, and chili swirl outside of the stadium. They discuss the surprise meeting that morning with Seamus. Amanda is pissed at Brian for not telling her Seamus was coming to town. Amanda shares that Brian and Seamus have been keeping in touch throughout the years, and that Brian is sitting with Seamus at the game.

Marianne takes off her sunglasses, displaying a small bruise. She openly confesses what happened the previous night with Andrew, not revealing that Seamus witnessed it. Amanda touches the bruise gingerly. She's so angry that uncharacteristically, she can't speak, which scares Marianne. Marianne reassures her that the behavior just started, and they are going through counseling. Amanda hugs her and gives her encouragement, sharing additional choice words about Andrew. Marianne, for the first time, publicly agrees.

Marianne and Amanda join the tailgate parties, bumping into various friends before they finally find Brian and Seamus. Brian and Amanda go through their usual routine of giving each other shit. Brian gets caught momentarily looking at a couple of coeds, setting Amanda off. "Oh, you like what you see? Go ahead. Look a little longer," she says.

"You know no one comes close to your radiant beauty."

She shoots him a stare worthy of Medusa. "Bullshit, Callaghan."

The four old friends share a laugh and a beer. Marianne's having a hard time keeping her eyes off Seamus. She's curious about, and attracted to, both his demeanor and his aura. Brian and Amanda talk with other friends, trying to give the two of them some space.

"I never had a chance to tell you how sorry I was—how sorry I am about Paddy."

"Thank you," Seamus says. "He really liked you, you know."

"Whatever happened to Angus?"

"He passed away while I was fishing Badger Creek east of Glacier National Park. A pretty nice way to go." A moment passes as Seamus reflects on his old pal.

Just like during the special year they spent together, Seamus and Marianne aren't distracted by anything around them. As Seamus takes a pull from his beer, Colin comes up behind Marianne and gives her a long hug. Seamus's eyes immediately focus on him.

"Did you reach Rebecca? Is Charlie sleeping any better?" Marianne says to Colin. "Oh, excuse me. Seamus, this is my son, Colin. He has my one-and-a-half-year-old grandson back at home in Seattle—they don't spend a lot of time separated. Colin, this is Seamus, an old friend of mine."

As they shake hands, Seamus squeezes Colin's hand as if to extract every molecule from his being. The two men, the same height and stature, look directly into each other's familiar eyes. As Marianne watches, her pride shifts to a chilly sensation. What she's previously considered is now obvious. Colin fills Marianne in on his conversation with his wife—the baby is doing fine, but Rebecca's ready for him to come home. He and Seamus hit it off immediately, and the small group is soon laughing and joking.

In the middle of their conversation, Andrew and a friend

stroll up. It takes Andrew a moment to place Seamus, but after the introductions are made, he recognizes his wife's old college flame. Seamus is cordial as he shakes Andrew's hand and asks how he's doing.

"Doing great—same old, same old. I'm sure Marianne filled you in. I'm in real estate. Business is strong, I gotta tell you. I can't go into details—you know how it is—but I've got a couple big developments in the works." He puts his arm around Marianne, marking his territory.

She cringes, half at the contact and half at how embarrassingly intimidated he is by Seamus. She waits a moment and then ducks out from under his arm as furtively as possible.

"You find a ride home last night?" Seamus asks. "I saw you at the Depot pretty late."

Marianne attempts to hide her smile. Andrew's feeling more and more uncomfortable.

"How about you? What have you been up to all these years?" Andrew says. "That hip heal up?"

"Yep. Still just working in the mining business."

"Good ole Butte boy, still digging in the dirt." Andrew relaxes a bit, pleased to be beating Seamus in his career and status.

Seamus refuses to play the one-upmanship game, continuing his cryptic facade. Brian comes to the rescue, yelling for him to return to the football game. Seamus excuses himself, Amanda picks up Marianne, and Andrew returns to his friends. As the ROTC cannon fires to alert the tailgaters to return to the stadium, Marianne looks up at Mount Sentinel, contemplating the unexpected turn of events. Marianne has seen a glimmer of hope.

✳✳✳

After the homecoming game, Seamus heads to Amanda and Brian's home. They sit in the backyard, catching up, joking around, and getting the inside scoop on old friends. Even though Brian and Seamus usually talk on the phone or over the Internet several times a year, they haven't actually seen each other in decades.

Seamus enjoys his chance to finally meet the Callaghan family. After many attempts to have children, Amanda and Brian eventually adopted three beautiful daughters. In an argument for nurture over nature, the Callaghan children are all loud and boisterous, much like their mother. The oldest is a college freshman, and the other two are in high school. The girls tell their dad they are going to visit friends. "Stay away from the three Ds!" Mother Hen Amanda yells through the kitchen window. The girls throw her familiar disapproving glares.

Seamus gives Brian a quizzical look. "Drinks, drugs, and dicks," says Brian.

The girls kiss their dad goodbye and troop back into the kitchen to Amanda.

"I definitely know why people have their children in their 20s instead of their 40s," Brian says. "I have about half the energy I used to."

Seamus watches the interaction of the loving family, wondering what he's missed. Brian starts up the barbecue and cracks open a couple of beers.

As the afternoon deepens into evening, they move their conversation inside. Seamus is vague to the point of secrecy about the details of his life. When Amanda tries to press him, he cracks a smile and jokes. "Telephone, tel-Amanda—no one knows where certain information may end up."

"Oh, come on. If you won't say what you do, at least tell us where you're living."

"I'm in the mining business, which takes me around the world. I'm in transit a lot. But I've got a little place in Chicago."

Seamus turns the questions around—Brian discusses his law practice, and Amanda, a successful financial consultant, discusses the markets. Seamus asks her several intelligent questions and listens intently to her answers, vetting her financial competence. The group eases back into old rhythms; they're relaxed and laughing. When Amanda brings up Marianne's situation, Seamus downplays his interest, saying he's sorry things aren't going as planned. "I definitely missed an opportunity," he says. "Andrew sure is the same large-and-in-charge dude."

Brian walks back into the room with more beer. He raises his bottle. "Here's to growing up with the six Bs: Buffett, Billy, Bob, Boston, the Boss, and, of course, Bongo." Seamus and Brian share a laugh at their ex-roommate Moose's expense. Amanda yells from the kitchen, "What about Benatar?"

***

On the Tuesday after homecoming weekend, Marianne and Amanda meet at a coffee shop downtown. Marianne's in jeans; Amanda struggles with her business attire, readjusting her Spanx. She's running family errands between appointments. They share small talk and check each other's daily agendas. Amanda says, "So are we gonna talk about the elephant in the room? What was it like seeing Seamus again?"

"I just keep thinking about being 19, you know? I don't know how my dreams and priorities became so messed up."

"I don't know about that," Amanda says. "You're a damn fine ER doctor, and you've got two amazing kids and a gorgeous grandson. I'd say you're doing pretty well."

"I'm OK, Amanda. I don't need a pep talk."

"I'm not pep talking. Anyway, Seamus looks good, huh? It's too bad that hip injury caught up with him—I thought it had healed up OK."

"What did Brian say about him? I can't believe they've been in touch this whole time."

"Tell me about it. I could just about kill him for never saying anything all these years." Amanda sips her coffee. "Brian is being very weird about the whole situation. They must communicate with a sixth sense or something. But Seamus seems happy and successful. He's working and living abroad somewhere, in addition to the States. He said something about Chicago, but I'm not sure that was entirely accurate."

"Saturday night, the two of them drove out to the Lumberjack Saloon and didn't get back till late. Then Seamus was up early, grabbed a cup of coffee, and drove to Butte. He said he was gonna say hello to some friends, go to church, and deal with some type of unfinished business. Something weird was going on. Saturday night, Brian was really excited, like his long-lost brother had shown up again. Then, on Sunday morning, he seemed off. Depressed and removed. Probably the combination of a hangover and Seamus leaving. It was just strange."

Amanda glances at her watch. "Oh shit," she says. "I completely forgot to pick up the dog food. I gotta get across town and back before this meeting starts." She reaches into her purse, pulls out a business card, and hands it to Marianne. The white card includes only an international phone number. Amanda tells her Seamus wanted her to have it. Amanda hugs Marianne and gives her a wistful look before hustling out the door, saying, "Shit, shit, shit."

Marianne laughs, picks up her book, reads a bit, and then puts her reading glasses and the book down on the table. She fiddles with the card and looks into space, thanking the waiter as he refills her coffee cup.

***

That night, Marianne's at her desk, paying bills. Andrew naps on the couch after a taxing evening of channel surfing. She stealthily pulls Seamus's business card out of her purse and looks at it for a long time. She glances over her shoulder and then grabs her mobile phone, takes a deep breath, and texts a short note to Seamus: "It was wonderful to see you this weekend. I'd really like to keep in touch and find out what has been happening in your life. It seems like I did all the talking this time around—well, me and my obnoxious husband. I'm sorry about that. Thanks again."

The next morning, Marianne quickly fixes breakfast for Polly while Andrew rattles off several errand requests for the day. Marianne is late for her shift. As she rushes for the door, she notices her mobile phone is lit up. The screen displays the arrival of a text message.

Marianne pauses and pulls the message up. Seamus's note is brief: "Hello. Nice to see a note from you so soon. You were up late last night. I would enjoy keeping in touch." She turns the phone off, smiles, and heads to the hospital with a new skip in her step.

Van Blakely

Chapter 14

The texting between the old friends continues for a couple of weeks. Marianne finds herself laughing more frequently and looking forward to checking her phone between her shifts every day. Marianne texts Seamus to say that Andrew is heading to Seattle with Polly the following week to visit his relatives and Colin's family. She realizes she can't remember the last time she had a weekend to herself, and she's looking forward to it. She receives a surprisingly immediate answer: "How about an adventure? Why don't you meet me in Big Sky on Friday night? I'm in Atlanta next week. The aspens are beautiful this time of year. I'll meet you at the J Bar T at seven."

Marianne is stunned. She doesn't know what to do. She heads to work and then later meets Andrew for lunch, which brings home her current situation. That afternoon, between a couple of patients, Marianne grabs her phone and types, "Yes." She tells Andrew she is heading to Billings for some continuing-education courses.

***

The J Bar T country roadhouse bar and grill is hopping on Friday night, its log benches and booths crowded and noisy. Marianne hesitates for just a moment before telling the hostess she's meeting someone. The hostess seats her in a booth. She watches as a patron in well-worn cowboy boots exits his barstool with a Rainier bottle in his left hand. Marianne's eyes light up as Seamus heads to their table, his movements casual and confident despite his limp. She stands and gives him a quick hug. Seamus apologizes for not seeing her come in. After some casual banter, Marianne orders a glass of wine, and Seamus requests another Rainier longneck. Marianne continues to vacillate between nervousness and excitement, having faithfully kept her wedding vows up to this point.

Both Marianne and Seamus are timid as they begin to get reacquainted. Seamus starts with the questions; Marianne briefly runs through her time in Seattle and her family and career. Seamus asks about the life of an ER doctor, and Marianne is happy to fill in the details, until she catches herself talking too much again. She is much more anxious to learn about Seamus's life.

Their dinners are delivered, and Seamus begins to share his history. Just before Paddy's death, Seamus finished school at Montana Tech in Butte. After Paddy passed away, Seamus left for Notre Dame, where he finished his MBA, knowing Paddy would be more than pleased. He jointly completed law school, draining all of his limited inheritance. During graduate school, he interned at the Chicago Board of Trade, learning the commodity markets and networking within the industry. With his mining upbringing, mining engineering degree, MBA, law degree, and Chicago contacts, his plan was to enter the mining business, but that plan changed abruptly when he was recruited into the American clandestine service—the CIA. Given his education and physical abilities, they aggressively pursued him, agreeing to pay his student loan debt and provide extensive flight training in exchange for work as an undercover operative. He'd grown up listening to Paddy's views on the importance of serving one's country, so he chose that alternative path. He traveled the world for years. His most intense times were spent as an undercover sniper in Uganda and Libya, providing intelligence during the Ugandan genocide and the ascension of Muammar Gaddafi.

The waitress brings them after-dinner coffee and they share a dessert as Seamus continues to recount his life. Marianne listens in shock. Seamus shares his uncertainty about his choice—he witnessed human beings at their worst. After nearly a decade of service, he returned to his original plan, becoming involved in numerous global copper and diamond mining operations. Seamus downplays his accomplishments, choosing not to share too much information too soon. He tells her he primarily resides in Chilean Patagonia and Antwerp, Belgium, the hub of the world's diamond industry. He also kept the Big Hole ranch, his promise to Angus.

"You know, Marianne, I'm just a third-generation miner from Butte. I'm a guy who grapples in the mud and mire for diamonds because diamonds are not found in polished stones. They are made." Marianne gently smiles, understanding his ambiguous yet metaphoric reference.

"And are you married?" Marianne asks, looking him straight in the eye.

"Once, to an Argentinian debutante. We were married for eight years. No kids, unfortunately. I was struggling with PTSD for a lot of our marriage. And all the travel wasn't exactly healthy for the relationship. We lived a really extravagant, jet-set kind of life, and ultimately, that just didn't feed my Butte-boy soul." Seamus takes a pull on his beer. "We're all looking for someone to ease our worried minds, aren't we? Some of us find it; some of us don't."

Marianne leans back in her seat, somewhat blown away by his story, keenly aware of the hint of sadness in his eyes. She fondles her locket for a moment and then says, "I'm sorry about what happened back in college. I should've stuck by you—I just couldn't handle it all back then."

"You made the best decision you could with the information you had at that time; it's a waste of time to hope for a better past. Besides, I'm the only one to blame. It's so obvious I pushed you away. Those college years can be so much fun and so innocent, yet at the same time, some of the experiences are so cruel and humbling. I wonder if the emotional growth is ultimately more important than the intellectual growth during those years." He gives a short laugh. "I'm not sure anyone should judge men between the ages of 15 and 25, since we're all pretty much peckerheads then, anyway. Young women deserve better."

Marianne laughs, and Seamus continues to make light of the situation that obviously redirected his life. "The difference in men is that the good men grow out of that stage," he says.

"I think that's true," Marianne says. She glances up as a country tune strikes up in the next room.

"Care to dance?" Seamus says. Together they head to the dance floor. (*Always on My Mind by Willie Nelson*)

When they return, Marianne says, "How's your hip? Did the old injury cause some arthritis?"

Seamus anticipated this question from a physician, and he responds neutrally. "The hip healed up nicely—I'm just waiting for some orthopedic information from my doctor. You're probably right—just arthritis."

***

The blinding morning sun glares through a plane window as the engine blares. (*The First Cut is the Deepest by Sheryl Crow*)

Marianne glances out the passenger window and then over at the small plane's pilot: Seamus. The rented Cessna 182 hums as Seamus rolls the plane into a Rocky Mountain canyon. It's a crisp champagne day, and the gold of the aspens and western larch is breathtaking. Marianne is happy to see that Seamus's teenage dream of flying has been realized. The US military trained him well.

After a glorious ride over the Gallatin Valley and Yellowstone Park, Seamus glides the single-engine bird to a nearly perfect landing. They taxi down the small Big Sky, Montana, runway and come to a stop at the airport hangars, next to a large private Boeing business jet. As they exit the rented four-seat single-engine prop plane and walk toward the quiet hangars, Marianne comments on the beautiful private aircraft, not recognizing the Chilean flag under the pilot's-side window. "What does it say under there?" she says. They get a little closer, and she makes out the words *Needle's Eye*. Seamus ignores the reference, choosing to comment only on the interesting play on words. As Marianne and Seamus walk away, an Hispanic man peers out of the cockpit.

***

A waitress presents a bottle of wine to Marianne and Seamus, the moonlight illuminating Lone Peak in the window behind her. The two friends sample the exquisite vintage and reflect on the day. After a sip or two, Marianne begins to tear up. She opens up more than she did the night before. She talks about her wonderful children, her passionless marriage, and the lack of personal direction in her life. "I feel like I gave up my freedom for security, and in the end, I just lost them both." She speaks of the pressures of the bad relationship, the effects it has had on her children, and the many things she feels guilty about.

Seamus says, "Having matriculated"—he pauses and smiles— "from traditional structured religion, I have never and will never buy into the guilt and fear preached from any pulpit. To me, it's all very simple: faith, hope, love, forgiveness, sacrifice, and free will. The Good Book simply coaches us to believe in a Supreme Being, love and forgive our neighbors, take care of the downtrodden, and live lives serving others.

"It reminds me of what my favorite Chicago lawyer friend says: law is very simple. Law is the search for determining what is right for the good of an individual as well as for a society. When what is right is not well defined, that's when lawyers are supposed to help define its identity. Unfortunately, the legal profession has lost sight of this concept. The law is supposed to be the lube oil of society's engine. Instead, it has become the sludge. I'm not trying to preach and tell you what to do Marianne, but don't let your guilt become the sludge of your soul.

"Where does it say we are required to live with our past mistakes our entire lives? The key spiritual messages of any religion are forgiveness and selflessness. So what if you've made mistakes? Take the time to heal the wounds, learn from them, and then get on with life." Despite the heavy subject matter, Seamus keeps his tone light. "Remember the Eagles song 'Already Gone'? I like to think about that last verse—'So often times it happens, we live our lives in chains, when we never really know we have the keys.'"

After dinner, they take a walk in the autumn night. Marianne shares that she is haunted by the stigma of divorce. Seamus, having gone through it, shares his perspective. "There's a fine line between working on something too long and simply cutting bait. Sometimes, fortunately or unfortunately, freedom has to win out."

"I feel like I'm at that point now," Marianne says.

"The beauty of freedom is that each of us has the opportunity to cut our own diamond the way we wish." Seamus laughs at himself a bit. "I know the world is full of diamond clichés, but to a miner, it symbolizes something unique. A raw diamond often looks no more pristine than a simple pebble.

"I like to think of it like this: A pure diamond offers perfect refraction and clarity, and symbolizes the way we should live—to live simply, think clearly, and free your mind of worldly possessions. Like diamonds, we all possess different characteristics, colors, and clarity. Only you can decide what you want exposed, whether it's how flashy or subtle we wish to appear, as well as how many flaws we wish to share or expose. None of us is a perfect diamond, but we can take the best we have and do the most with it."

"Well, I've certainly done well at exposing my flaws," joked Marianne.

"Haven't we all," smiled Seamus. "But the flaws are sometimes what make diamonds most valuable—and what provide them personal sentiment. Is a near-perfect, expensive diamond purchased in a shopping mall worth more to somebody than an heirloom from a loved one, passed down through a family for generations, whatever its size or quality?"

"The heirloom, of course," said Marianne, "although I can think of a few people who'd choose the flashy store diamond."

"That says pretty much all you need to know about them, doesn't it?" asked Seamus. "Be suspicious of the unblemished life. The true value of a diamond is in the feeling and dreams that it carries with it."

He continued, "Think of your life as your diamond. The natural flaws, the scratches of the environment it has endured, and the rough edges that haven't yet been perfected determine its shape. But you are the only one who can determine your innate value." Seamus pauses. "Malcolm Forbes said, 'Diamonds are nothing more than chunks of coal that stuck to their jobs.'"

"Ha! That's funny."

"Marianne, you have fought the good fight, my friend—you have faced and fought your challenges. You have stuck to your job."

When they reach Marianne's cabin, she invites him in. Seamus takes her in his arms, looking deep into her eyes, gauging her emotional state. "Yes, I'll come in. And by the way, I'll be here when you wake up."

Marianne smiles, remembering.

The next morning, Seamus helps Marianne load her car, struggling with one of her bags as he fights to get his left leg to cooperate. He never complains, and Marianne doesn't draw attention to it. They give each other a long, passionate kiss, sure their paths will cross in the near future. "What time does your flight take off?" Marianne asks.

"I've got to return the rental truck, and I wanted to cruise the area a bit before heading home."

After a final embrace, Marianne drives away, looking in her rearview mirror. Seamus jumps into the truck, rolls the window down, and takes a deep breath of the mountain air, as if to make a memory.

Instead of following Marianne toward the Gallatin County Airport, he makes a left turn, returning to the smaller Big Sky airstrip. After parking the truck next to the hangar, he walks toward the Cessna 182 that he flew with Marianne. As it taxis toward him, Seamus crosses his arms as if to show his displeasure. Once the engine is cut, Seamus strolls over to the pilot's door. When the door opens, Seamus jokes, "I knew you couldn't resist seeing me flying through these mountains, could you?"

The handsome Hispanic pilot exits the plane, laughing, and Seamus throws his arm around him. "Are you driving today, or am I?"

Together, they take a step onto the stairway of the *Needle's Eye*.

✶✶✶

Marianne gazes out the window during the hospital staff meeting. Her colleagues notice how quiet she's been. She remains introspective as she deals with minor ER events throughout the morning, catching up on some paperwork. After many years, she has once again been bitten by the love bug.

Van Blakely

Chapter 15

In his law office, Brian slams the phone down, muttering, "That son of a bitch." He then calls for his assistant while he sifts through his paper-infested desk. She hurriedly walks in and fields his question about a legal file that needs to be picked up. Brian explains that a final alteration is required on the document.

"The packet is at the front desk, waiting for the courier," she says.

Brian rushes to the front desk and snatches the document. As he starts back upstairs, he catches a familiar figure out of the corner of his eye: Marianne is standing in the reception area. He's momentarily surprised by her presence, and then he smiles quickly, knowing what must have brought her in. "Marianne," he says, "what an unexpected pleasure." He turns to the receptionist, instructing her to hold his calls for the next couple of hours. "Come on up," he says, putting his arm around her and escorting her to his office. Marianne's awakening is now public.

Andrew and Marianne's separation and divorce proceedings are ugly. Brian is anxious to bury Andrew. At first, Andrew blames Marianne's newfound strength on the influence of Amanda, but it doesn't take long until he discovers that Marianne didn't travel to Billings after all. Battle lines are drawn. Andrew makes public his new relationship with a local young upscale real estate agent, but his ego suffers since it's well known that he wasn't the one to initiate the breakup. He is poised to fight to the end, and spends countless hours doing his best to hide assets.

Marianne begins a new life on her own, enjoying her children and throwing herself into Thanksgiving and pre-Christmas activities. She works to rebuild her self-esteem, slowly beginning to treasure her earthy independence. She takes a trip to Polson, driving past Esther's cottage and taking a long walk up to their wishing tree. She's searching to find her true center—it's been absent for many years.

***

Seamus calls Marianne a few weeks before Christmas to wish her a happy holiday.

"To be honest, I thought I would hear from you sooner," Marianne says. "Why didn't you call?"

Seamus pauses and then dodges the question.

They catch up briefly, with Marianne giving a CliffsNotes version of her divorce proceedings. After a moment's quiet, Seamus says, "So what are your plans after Christmas? I know you'll probably want to be home with your kids for the holiday, but I'd like to take you on a special New Year's trip if you're game. Shouldn't take more than 10 days or so. What do you think? I'd love to spend New Year's Eve with you."

Marianne runs over her schedule—she's already scheduled a well-deserved vacation for those weeks, knowing Polly would be in Seattle visiting Colin and her nephew.

"I would love to," she says. He tells her he'll take care of the travel arrangements and will e-mail her later with the details.

***

In Atlanta, Seamus looks intently at the Emory University doctor telling him his medical fate. (*I've Been Searchin' So Long by Chicago*) Even though he feared the outcome was pretty much sealed, aggressively reviewing exploratory and holistic alternatives had kept his hopes intact. He exits the doctor's office and stands next to a framed picture of a red-tailed hawk. Stunned and numb, Seamus is somehow still able to crack a smile at the irony and synchronicity of the moment, thinking back to the lunch he shared with the predatory bird in the Big Hole Valley. Today, he muses, he's the unfortunate mouse.

Outside, he's met by his pilot, who escorts him to the Boeing business jet. Seamus instructs him to head to Seattle. He settles into his jet, and a flight attendant hands him a beverage, sensing his pensive state. As the jet takes off, he looks out across the Atlanta skyline, his mind on his failed exploration efforts and his sure demise. The attendant pours him another glass of Jack Daniels on the rocks, this time leaving the bottle.

***

Dressed in a long raincoat and escorted by another man dressed in a trench coat, Seamus stands in the Puget Sound drizzle and watches from afar as Colin laughs and glides across the field of a flag football game in the Green Lake area. Colin is light-hearted, and it's clear he's well-liked by his teammates. Seamus can see them cracking jokes and poking fun at each other.

After the game, Colin retreats to his wife and son, and holds his son up to the sky, making the toddler giggle. His wife gathers their belongings as Colin lifts his son onto his shoulders. The couple holds hands as they walk along the lake path toward their modest home. Seamus unconsciously takes a few steps in their direction and then catches himself. A smile comes to his face as he watches the young family disappear around a curve.

The man in the trench coat approaches Seamus.

"Got what you needed?" Seamus says. The man nods, removing and displaying a plastic evidence bag from his coat. Having reverted to his clandestine days, Seamus takes a deep breath and then says, "Let's head back to Boeing Field and venture down to Portland."

***

Marianne arrives at the Missoula airport per Seamus's instructions. Since he has informed her that the flight departs at 6:30 a.m., Marianne assumes it must be the early morning Delta flight. She stops at the Delta counter and then the United and Alaska Air ticket counters. No ticket is reserved. Carrying her bags around the terminal, she wonders what happened to the plan. She is approached by a young Hispanic man in a black trench coat. "Are you Dr. Wells?" he asks.

"I am. Can I help you?"

"Please follow me, ma'am. I'm with Mr. McElroy."

As they make their way through the terminal, she runs into some acquaintances. All parties are curious about each other's respective destinations. One couple tells Marianne they're headed to Kauai. To their surprise, Marianne tells them she's not sure where she's going.

She continues to follow the man, who takes her outdoors.

They walk through the winter snow toward a black SUV. The man opens the car door and then whisks her across the tarmac toward the other side of the airport.

"I'm sorry, sir," she says. "Where is it we're headed?"

"We'll be at the hangar momentarily."

Exiting the SUV at the large hangar, Marianne stops for a moment. In front of her, is the *Needle's Eye*. Marianne recognizes she's been deceived. She walks into the hangar, where Seamus is pouring a cup of coffee. They give each other a casual hug, and Marianne asks, "What are you up to?"

The young man, this time without his jacket, returns with another man; both are sporting airplane captain attire. He asks Seamus if he can load the luggage, and Seamus nods. Marianne accepts the coffee he offers her. Seamus looks her straight in the eye and says, "Are you ready for an adventure?"

Marianne holds his gaze. "You bet."

With warm drinks in hand, they exit the hangar. Marianne, grinning, can hardly contain her excitement as they board the exquisite aircraft. As the plane begins to taxi down the tarmac, Marianne laughs with anticipation.

"Why didn't you greet me? I thought I was being kidnapped for a second there."

"Missoula's still a small town, and I'm not your husband."

She nods, appreciating the forethought. "Next question. What's up with the *Needle's Eye*?"

"I'm just trying to deliver camels."

Marianne scrunches her eyes, having no clue what he's talking about, but recognizing his choice to be mysterious. The plane blasts off, turning to the south through the cloudy morning sky.

***

Hours later, the *Needle's Eye* (*Where the Streets Have No Name by U2*) drops down through the clouds, skirting across the subtropical rainforest and suddenly breaking out over the beautiful Pacific Ocean. The plane turns, making its approach toward a small landing strip. Marianne looks out the window and then turns back smiling, looking to Seamus as if to thank him. A couple of wonderful days in Panama lie in front of them.

After they unload, an open Jeep speeds the two old friends to Seamus's quaint, but luxurious, beach cabana. Marianne has only witnessed such tropical beauty in magazines—it's nothing like the resorts her family would sometimes visit. Touring the high-end neighborhood and adjoining resort, Seamus and Marianne soak up the sun, enjoying each other's company, boat drinks, walks on the beach, and a beautiful dinner. During the meal, Seamus and Marianne are no longer interested in discussing Marianne's transition.

The next morning, the couple enjoys a catered breakfast; a feast of fruit, juices, coffee, and pastries are displayed in front of them. "You feel like leaving the campus for a few hours?" Seamus says.

Marianne shoots him a curious look and gives a "Why not?" shrug, game for anything. "Can you speak any Spanish?" she asks.

"Well, I know beer is *cerveza*, and bathroom is *baño*. And one other thing: 'Can I date your seester?'" Seamus impishly grins.

Marianne shakes her head—she knows a little bit of Paddy will always be in Seamus's heart and soul.

After breakfast, they jump into an open-topped Jeep and head into the native town. The deeper into the town they get, the more uncomfortable Marianne becomes. The Americanized resort compound seemed hospitable and secure compared to the poverty she is now witnessing. At the moment she feels the most uncomfortable, Seamus stops the vehicle and exits. Marianne remains seated, nervous to join him. He smiles, motioning for her to walk with him.

As Marianne and Seamus walk through the neighborhood, several locals follow their every move; Marianne is restless. When she and Seamus turn a corner, a group of men seated next to a dilapidated bar stand up and approach them. Just as Marianne begins to tug on Seamus's arm, one of the men greets Seamus, welcoming Senor Mac. Seamus launches into a fluent Spanish dialogue with the rough-looking men. It's all smiles, jokes, handshakes, and eventual hugs. The men soon wish the couple farewell and return to their seats by the tavern.

Seamus throws Marianne a reassuring glance, and they continue walking. Soon, they come to a quaint and simple mission, which includes an orphanage, a women's shelter, a micro bank, expansive gardens and greenhouses, and a senior center. As they approach the entrance, a young child excitedly shouts into the traditional, yet modern, structure. Seemingly within nanoseconds, a horde of children streams out the door, running full tilt toward the couple. Seamus kneels to accept their loving hugs. They quickly engage him in Spanish dialogue and finally take Seamus and Marianne by the hand and escort them into the Catholic enclave.

Inside, they are greeted by an excited nun. (*Give a Little Bit by Supertramp*) Seamus and Marianne help serve lunch to the festive children, playfully bantering back and forth. Marianne can only look to Seamus with quiet admiration, noting his selfless humility. After several hours, which feel like minutes to Marianne, the couple retreats to the coastline. Sitting by the sea that evening, Seamus turns to Marianne. "So, which was the better day?" he asks.

She thinks back over their busy hours and the children she met. "What a silly question," she says. Seamus nods in agreement.

***

The next morning, they again board the *Needle's Eye*, heading for Seamus's true home, the Chilean Lake District. After several long hours, the jet descends into an Andean valley, and one of South American's most beautiful regions comes into sight. It's summer in the Southern Hemisphere, and the area is lush. Seamus's small entourage escorts them to his country estate north of Puerto Veras.

Marianne is blown away. They exit the plane and then walk through a large hangar. Marianne notices a Cessna 182 similar to the plane at Big Sky parked in the hangar, but she is more interested in the small black-and-gold Russian MiG fighter jet parked next to it. She stops, looking closely at the high-tech fighter and then up at Seamus. "Yours?"

He nods, a little sheepish. "One of my Chilean general buddies pulled a little favor for me."

"Have you buzzed the Big Hole lately?"

Seamus laughs, and Marianne grins, knowing she is on the greatest adventure of her life.

Over the next week, Seamus and Marianne tour his adopted homeland, flying to some mammoth copper mines he's involved with. The Butte mine is dwarfed by the size of these operations. In Seamus's office, Marianne notices the framed military and mining photographs of Seamus's great-grandfather that, several decades earlier, adorned Paddy's bar. Seamus tells her more about his global mining and railroad operations, primarily in Africa, Australia, and the Andes. During several of his mining projects, he took equity stakes rather than cash. Seamus explains how mining has changed, with many countries switching to privately-owned entities rather than state-run operations. Being involved with different projects in their respective infancies afforded him the opportunity to pick the most promising projects.

They spend time exploring the countryside and culture, taking in the best of the country. It doesn't take long for Marianne to recognize what has kept him in this part of the world—the environment surprisingly mimics western Montana, especially the fly-fishing. On Sunday, they attend Mass in a beautiful old cathedral. Marianne quickly notices Seamus's rock-star status within the community. The people view him with not only awe, but also respect for his spiritual maturity. After the service, they are greeted by another group of adoring children from the attached orphanage and small clinic. A priest welcomes Marianne with open arms, conversing in Spanish with Seamus.

After the conversation, Seamus takes Dr. Wells into the small, modern hospital. During a tour led by the attending physician, Marianne is fascinated by the hospital's high-end, high-tech capabilities. The doctor gives all the credit to Seamus, who downplays the recognition, concentrating on some rambunctious children.

At that moment, a man rushes into the hospital with his daughter in his arms. Her face is blue—she's in dire need of medical attention. Acting on instinct, Dr. Wells jumps into the fray. As she and the other doctor discuss the situation, the staff notes Marianne's intensity and professionalism; her presence is clearly appreciated. After some tense moments, the doctors diagnose the problem and are able to stabilize the little girl's condition. Meanwhile, Seamus watches, recognizing he has made the right decision, completing his final vetting.

Their last destination is the southern tip of Chile—Tierra del Fuego and the Strait of Magellan. It's a desolate place, weathered and violent, overlooking the earth's two largest oceans' violent convergence. Seamus and Marianne peer into the distance in a vain attempt to catch a glimpse of Antarctica 500 miles to the south. It's a lonely, but spiritual moment. As they huddle next to a rock to evade the strong breeze, Seamus asks if she's had a good time. She looks longingly at him, not needing to speak to say thank you. Then, out of nowhere, Dr. Wells asks, "It was your right hip in college, wasn't it?"

Seamus manages a forced smile, biting his lip. "Yes."

"Do you want to talk about it?"

A surprising, comfortable glow comes to Seamus's face. "No." There's a restless pause as Seamus looks out over the sea. "My smile is my makeup."

After a pensive moment, Seamus goes on. "True happiness is generated and transformed when a human being's evolving and maturing inner peace travels through the soul's prism, allowing one to witness the world through the optical lens of another and genuinely place another's soul before one's own. It's about empathy and then charity. If you choose to give the gospels of any religion a chance, their respective and consistent message plainly encourages us to follow a similar path: to simply and honestly love each other while taking care of the downtrodden, gifts bestowed upon each of us by grace. All you have is your health and love. And when you no longer have your health …" Seamus, for the first time, begins to choke up, but he quickly catches himself. "All you can do is give." The two homesteaders from the American frontier huddle on the shoreline.

The *Needle's Eye* returns Marianne to Montana.

Chapter 16

An old coffeepot percolates on a woodstove in a log cabin. A hand holding a rag cautiously grips the handle and pours the steaming liquid into an old blue metal camping coffee cup. Seamus limps over to a wooden table, where he sits alone, eating his breakfast of bacon and eggs. He appears pensive this morning as he periodically looks out the window at the sun finally appearing over the mountains. Once he's finished with his breakfast, he makes his way over to the old sink, where he methodically washes and dries the dirty dishes. He then carefully places them in their designated places in weathered overhanging cupboards. He drapes the wet towel over a bar and makes his way outside to a waiting rocking chair on the covered porch.

It's a beautiful early June morning in the Big Hole Valley. It's so green one would think they were in Ireland but for the surrounding rugged Rocky Mountains. Summer has finally arrived in the high Montana valley. The birds chirp playfully, and the wildflowers welcome the sunshine as they glisten in the morning dew. He rocks with his coffee cup in hand, his mind full of treasured memories from his youth in this valley, when life seemed less complicated and more innocent. As he finishes his last sip of cowboy coffee, a deluxe dually double-cab pickup pulls up in front of the old cabin. Seamus's Chilean pilots exit the vehicle, and they greet him as he loads into the front passenger seat.

The three men joke and laugh as they meander up the Highway 43 cutoff toward the town of Anaconda and turn northwest on Highway 1, which takes them past Georgetown Lake and drops down into the Flint Creek drainage. As they near the small town of Philipsburg, they turn off to a tiny airstrip, where the *Needle's Eye* is prominently parked. The men exit the pickup, talking and enjoying each other's company. They walk past the exquisite jet, examining it as they make their way to a lone hangar across the tarmac.

Once they reach the building, Seamus pauses and says, "Probably gonna piss off the feds today."

The pilots nod and smile. One walks over to the hangar and

enters a security code to open the automatic door. As the massive door rolls open, the impeccable black-enamel reconstructed MiG fighter jet stands ready for departure. Seamus and the pilots methodically move the jet out of its home, going through the necessary preflight procedures. Eventually, Seamus, with some help from his friends, climbs up into the cockpit and continues the process. A small Mighty Mouse decal adorns the side of the plane just below the cockpit window, where a combat pilot's call sign is generally located.

Seamus starts up the fighter and begins to move down the tarmac. On the runway, before takeoff and after speaking with air traffic control in Salt Lake City, he reaches into his flight bag. He fumbles to put away his Wise River Bar baseball hat and his Ray-Ban flight sunglasses and eventually slips on a helmet, visor, and oxygen mask. He taxis the vintage fighter across the tarmac and comes to a halt at the end of the short runway. He pulls a worn cassette case out of the flight bag and slides the old Boston cassette tape into a recent modification: a cassette deck player. As the song (*Long Time by Boston*) cranks up on his headphones, he takes off at a steep angle, successfully launching the reconditioned MiG.

Seamus skims across the tree line, buzzing and entertaining the startled locals. He begins his tour of his beloved state of Montana, exploring numerous mountain ranges: the Bridgers, Crazies, Sapphires, Little Belts, Rubies, Tobacco Roots, Pioneers, Pintlers, and Beartooths. He looks down at the wild rivers: the Madison, Jefferson and Gallatin, Ruby, Boulder, Smith, Dearborn, and Beaverhead.

As Seamus flies over and through beautiful southwestern Montana, his life flashes before his eyes. His extraordinary life experiences finally deem him worthy of being Marianne's soulmate. The pictures in his mind are an alternating mosaic of the views from the cockpit and memories from his life after he left Butte: He is briefly watching a Notre Dame football game from a distant entrance with his backpack over his shoulder, yelling in the commodity trading pits of the Chicago Board of Trade, and exerting himself through basic training. Then two machete-wielding Ugandan soldiers are approaching a wailing woman huddled with her three children. As they raise their blood-drenched weapons, bullets pierce their respective foreheads, and a fully camouflaged Seamus emerges from the jungle. Next, an undercover Seamus watches helplessly as innocent Libyan college students are hanged in a city square. Seamus shivers nakedly in a corner as he struggles through PTSD. A hard-hatted Seamus operates a massive earth shovel. Seamus shakes hands with businessmen and politicians. Then Seamus is exchanging wedding vows, laying bricks while building a clinic, cresting the summit of a massive Andean peak, and kayaking past a melting glacier in Antarctica.

As the guitar solo commences, he quickly brings the plane to a nearly vertical position, and it screams up the side of the immense Granite Peak, Montana's highest peak, at 12,807 feet, in the Absaroka Beartooth Mountains. The snow quivers throughout the mountain canyons as the engines roar. As he barrels up the side of the colossal mountain, his mind continues to vacillate between his view from the cockpit and a distant memory: A delicate pair of hands carefully load a Mighty Mouse lunch box. The face of a young boy excitedly looks up at an adult as he and the adult walk to school. The young boy reaches up to kiss the adult's cheek and then skips toward his school in the background. The young boy shoots the adult a final adoring look. Seamus's beautiful mother calls to him, "Fly, Seamus. Fly!" Young Seamus puts out his arms as if he is a hawk cruising the Big Hole Valley. As the solo ends, the fighter shoots over the peak's apex, the morning sun sending its blinding rays into the cockpit. He brings the fighter to a hammerhead stall and slowly turns the fighter to come back to Earth.

A handsome young man in a tattered baseball cap drives a weathered tractor down a dirt road through a florescent-green field, enjoying another beautiful day in the Big Hole Valley. In an instant, his innocent morning turns into momentary chaos as he is buzzed by a jet on the deck. The young man gathers his wits, watching as the jet screams through the valley, tipping its wings to simultaneously say hello and goodbye, headed toward Butte.

The jet careens north toward the Mining City, and the Berkeley Pit appears on the horizon. As Seamus reaches the outskirts of the small city, he looks out his right window at the massive Our Lady of the Rockies statue that watches over the historic town, momentarily signaling his respect. The lyrics "I've got to keep on chasing a dream, though I may never find it" play as Seamus, his helmet and oxygen now discarded, looks down toward his instrument panel, where a treasured dream catcher hangs, given to him with love decades earlier. As the quickly approaching mountain reflects off his sunglasses, a tear rolls down his cheek. Seamus pile-drives the jet into the side of the open-pit copper mine, joining Paddy and his mother on the World's Richest Hill. The plane explodes at the base of the majestic natural cathedral. Local miners scurry as a second explosion engulfs the wreckage. As John Denver sang, Seamus has "talked to God and listened to the casual reply."

✳✳✳

In her scrubs, Marianne sits in the front pew of the hospital's chapel, holding her mobile phone. She has just received the tragic news from Brian. As she sobs, two hands are gently laid on her slumped shoulders. She wipes her eyes and finds Amanda next to her, once again her champion. Marianne is eventually able to force a smile, looking deeply into Amanda's sympathetic eyes.

Chapter 17

Several months later, at Brian's law firm, Marianne prepares for a hearing on her divorce case. When she walks into the firm's conference room, Brian and an attorney clad in blue pinstripes are conversing. She apologizes for disrupting the meeting and turns to go back to the lobby. "No, Marianne, stay—we were waiting for you to really get started. Here. Sit." Brian draws back a chair for her. "This is John O'Connor. He's in from Chicago—he was a close friend of Seamus. They were classmates at Notre Dame, and he served as Seamus's American counsel."

The Chicago lawyer shakes Marianne hand. "It's nice to finally meet you," he says before exchanging additional pleasantries. "I'm sorry to have to skip so quickly back to business, but that's what I'm here for. Seamus, as you may know, was very involved in the commodities and real estate markets." He begins to present Seamus's estate papers but is interrupted by a knock at the door. Another distinguished gentleman enters the room with a large security guard.

Marianne begins to fidget when she notices a briefcase locked to the guard's wrist. She furrows her brow, looking to Brian for some clarification. As usual, Marianne is noticeably uncomfortable with the strangers. Brian sends her a reassuring glance and smile.

Brian has been briefed in general and had a feeling the information might affect their divorce court hearing later that day. Mr. O'Connor resumes reading the contents of Seamus's estate. In a letter to Marianne, Brian, and Amanda accompanying his will, Seamus explains his reasons for the premeditated crash. The letter explains that Seamus was diagnosed with amyotrophic lateral sclerosis (ALS), or Lou Gehrig's disease, the devastating neurological disease with no cure. Seamus was sorry to deceive but didn't want his ailment to be the main subject of their final conversations. Marianne flashes back to the suicide patient she encountered months ago. She bows her head, understanding how scared and terrible Seamus must have felt.

Seamus knew something was seriously wrong prior to the

homecoming weekend and shared his concern with Brian at the Lumberjack Saloon. He wanted Marianne to have an unbiased familiarity with his life so she could make some future decisions. Seamus lived his entire life as an active, strong human being physically, mentally, emotionally, and spiritually. He chose not to leave the world in an invalid state, as Paddy had. He believed with his entire heart and soul that he should be able to dictate his destiny and legacy. Seamus has written, "Remember the words of Fogelberg: 'Death is there to keep us honest and constantly remind us we are free.' Live a life of compassion rather than fear." He ends the letter with a sincere request—one not to be taken lightly—regarding his unfinished quest, the quest of the *Needle's Eye*.

"Do you know exactly what he means by that?" Marianne asks the attorney.

"He and I used to talk about it quite a bit back in law school—the verses of Mark 10: 'I tell you the truth, anyone who will not receive the Kingdom of God like a little child will never enter it. Children, how hard it is to enter the Kingdom of God. It is easier for a camel to go through the eye of a needle than for a rich man to enter the Kingdom of God.'"

Marianne visualizes the words on the side of a plane as the attorney continues.

"Seamus asked for a favor. And I should let you know that contingencies are in place if you choose not to follow this path, which you should feel very comfortable in doing." He pauses and then continues. "Seamus's will designates the vast majority of his estate to select philanthropic organizations and reclamation efforts, the corpus to be invested and managed by three trustees—you two and Amanda—knowing you would be good stewards of the funds and understand the power and responsibility of charity. This includes his Panamanian and Chilean charities, Marianne, which you are familiar with."

Marianne nods.

"There are 18 additional scattered projects, located near each mining operation he was involved with, including a new facility in Butte—which is what he was working on during his final stop homecoming weekend."

The attorney reads Seamus's thoughts about his friend Brian.

The document makes provisions for buying him a new Mackenzie River fly-fishing boat and deeding him the family ranch down the Big Hole Valley. He asks Lucky to remember him when the fishing is good and writes, "A Montana ranch is a sanctuary for the soul." Brian, usually composed, is caught off guard and is visibly moved as he reflects on their friendship. He stares out the law firm's boardroom windows.

With the majority of the money going to the foundation, a smaller portion goes to Marianne. Seamus's will explains that the most important qualities of money are freedom and its ability to serve others. Her portion will not be less than $5 million, with no strings attached. The attorney estimates the estate's value, as of that morning, at approximately $717 million. Marianne is speechless.

The attorney asks Brian and Marianne if they are prepared to take on this endeavor, again explaining that alternative plans are in place should they choose not to pursue this responsibility. Stunned, Brian asks for some time to consult his financial adviser, Amanda, while Marianne requests some time to take care of some unfinished business. The Chicago attorney grants their requests.

Brian then introduces the distinguished gentleman who entered the room late, explaining he is from London. Marianne, obviously emotional and overwhelmed, stands and shakes his hand. The man explains, in a strong English accent, that he is an investigator from Lloyd's of London who received some interesting requests from Mr. McElroy. The gentleman begins talking about Mr. McElroy's estate. "A portion will go to your son, Colin." He hands her a paternity document acknowledging the now obvious. There is a pause in the room. "Please don't ask."

Brian and Marianne are stunned.

Next, the squire carefully hands Marianne the small piece of paper which has personal contact information of a young woman residing in Oregon, with a note underneath the information, in Seamus' handwriting, "Your locket isn't Pandora's Box anymore." Marianne is momentarily confused until she catches herself once again grasping her locket and its precious contents. She immediately reflects to an innocent pair of eyes looking up to her. The kind gentleman gently smiles and tells her the woman is expecting her call if Marianne chooses to make it her choice to pursue.

Lastly, the gentleman motions for the security guard to approach the group. The behemoth carefully places the fortified briefcase on the table and enters the electronic code to open the case. After lifting the lid, he retrieves a small wooden box and hands it to Marianne. She appraises the small box, noting a weathered "Ekati Mine—Northwest Territories" ink stamp. The gentleman signals for her to open it. When she does so, packing material and dirt fall onto the impeccable boardroom table; she tries to brush the debris off. She turns back to the box and picks out a rugged stone, looking to the group for some direction.

The gentleman grins. "It's an uncut paragon." When Marianne furrows her brow, confused, he continues. "The word paragon is typically recognized as a quality of excellence. However, it is also known as an unflawed diamond weighing at least 100 carats."

An ice-cold shiver goes down Marianne's spine, and she nearly drops the stone. She recalls her conversation with Seamus in Big Sky. Looking down again, she notices a note tucked in the bottom of the box. After unfolding the soiled piece of paper, she reads, "Just remember, I was there when you woke up." She smiles through her tears as she picks up her purse and pulls out her wallet. She opens the coin compartment and places Seamus's small piece of Montana quartz in the palm of her hand.

There is silence as the big picture unfolds for Marianne. The gentleman requests Marianne's permission to transport the stone to a reserved safety-deposit box at a local bank for her. Marianne looks for Brian's approval, which is quickly granted. Marianne sees that the attorney is moved by the unfolding events; she recognizes that he and Seamus were more than simply business associates.

"You were close during the years when we lost touch," she says. "How would you describe him, having known him for these decades?"

Mr. O'Connor glances out the window and then smiles. "Ben Franklin once said, 'There are three things extremely hard: steel, a diamond, and to know one's self.' He authentically knew himself."

He begins a story. After law school and before Seamus entered the service, they spent two months in Europe, two of the best months of his life. Even though they enjoyed everything Europe could provide, Seamus was adamant about seeing an ancient book in the British Museum in London.

In ancient India almost 2,500 years ago, Siddhartha, a rich prince, captivated the hearts and minds of his people, as would Jesus, who would not walk the Earth for another five centuries. He grew up surrounded by exorbitant wealth and luxury, yet after witnessing the suffering of many people, he recognized all humans will ultimately lose all possessions and people they cherish most. He abandoned his life of luxury to pursue a solitary quest to discover what causes suffering and how humans might put an end to it.

The wisdom gained by the prince was told via word of mouth for hundreds of years, revealing to people how to live lives filled with simplicity and compassion. He also espoused that when one is self-centered, he or she is off center from the essence of life itself. The ancient book conveys the pathway to compassion. The book teaches absolute wisdom while describing the extraordinary intelligence possessed by the people of ancient India. Eventually, these lessons were printed utilizing wood-block printing, thus making it the oldest-dated book in the world. Roughly a thousand years ago, the book ultimately reached Tibet and was translated into the Tibetan language. In Mongolia hundreds of years ago, the book was deemed so vital that each family kept a copy meticulously preserved on the altar in their home. Currently, the original copy is housed at the British Museum, dated AD 868, or 587 years before the Gutenberg Bible was assembled. The story and wisdom are obviously about the Buddha. What most people don't know is when the Indian and Tibetan title of the book is translated to English, the name of the ancient book is *The Diamond Cutter.*

"Was Seamus a Buddhist?" Marianne asks.

"No, he just had a little mystic in him. He was on a quest to find higher meaning and consciousness—searching for some level of enlightenment, which I believe he ultimately found. He knew how to live in the present moment, keeping physical form, inferiority, superiority, the past, and the future in the proper perspective. He knew that being centered is seldom related to being self-centered. He somehow discovered how to mine the world's energy, magic, and mystery.

"When Seamus and I were at Notre Dame, we chose to complete a theology course together. I don't remember anything from that class except one quote by a guy named Heschel, who said, 'When I was young, I admired clever people; now that I am older I admire kind people.'" He smiles, attempting to hold together his composure. "You all realize, right or wrong, Seamus spent his last days interviewing you—in return giving you the greatest gift in the world: the gift and spirit of giving, the key to true happiness."

***

An hour later, Brian and Marianne arrive late for the first divorce settlement meeting. They apologize to an aggravated Andrew and his counsel. The negotiations have continued to be messy. Andrew is only interested in the money. He is obsessed with the financial side of the settlement; Polly's well-being is an afterthought. Marianne can't bear to look at him and stares out the window.

Brian begins the discussion, explaining Dr. Sherman's—he purposely deletes the name Wells—desire to offer some major changes to the previous agreements. Andrew and his attorney are visibly upset, having thought they were close to a final settlement. Brian offers the house equity to Andrew, requiring no alimony, no child support, and no monetary settlement in return for custody of Polly. Andrew and his attorney are pleasantly dumbfounded. Andrew attempts to hide his excitement by voicing his concern for Polly's welfare, but the charade is over quickly. He doesn't even debate with counsel, telling him, "Take the deal!" Andrew can't sign the documents fast enough. Marianne continues to divert her eyes outside, her mind on the previous meeting. Brian hands Andrew's attorney a stack of papers.

As Brian and Marianne walk past Andrew, Marianne, realizing the time she has wasted, as well as the hypocrisy and hubris she endured, leans over and whispers, "I would like to buy a vowel."

***

Outside on the courthouse lawn, across from the law office, the maple leaves begin to turn. Amanda waits impatiently to hear the results. Amanda hugs Marianne, asking how things went. Marianne begins to shed happy tears. Brian gently cradles

Amanda's face in his hands, giving her a heartfelt kiss. He then gently strokes her hair, not needing to say a word. Amanda smiles, colorfully making light of everyone's emotions, acutely aware something big just happened.

The Callaghan SUV is parked backward so its tailgate is facing the courthouse sidewalk. Amanda is in charge of delivering one final item to Marianne. "We need to talk over some financial matters with you," Marianne says.

"Oh, that can wait," Amanda says. "Brian, you took forever. The new friend is restless."

Marianne looks up, curious.

Brian reaches into the SUV and hands Marianne a 12-week-old black Labrador puppy in a bright red collar with the name Angus on it. Marianne sits down on the courthouse lawn and begins to play with the pup.

"Are you OK, Mare?" Amanda says.

"I just need a few minutes." (*Will You Be There [in the Morning] by Heart*) The last time she felt this secure and confident was sitting on the dock at Flathead Lake surrounded by her family.

"Look at this. Can you believe the little shit?" Amanda says. Little Angus has relieved himself on her leather car seat.

"I'm on it," Brian says. He grabs some paper towels from the back of the vehicle and does his best to clean up the mess.

Marianne stands to embrace Amanda, holding the puppy close to her chest. As if prompted by Seamus's colorful spirit, the puppy carefully and accurately licks the tip of Amanda's nose, winning the final battle of wits.

The End

Music Index

The author encourages you to please consider supporting the charitable organizations referenced in the following links:

http://www.grizkidz.com
https://www.seattlenightwatch.org

And just for the pure pleasure of it, enjoy over 10 minutes of Boston performing "Foreplay/Long Time" at a concert to benefit "Boston Strong" via OneFundBoston.org.

https://bit.ly/2Avk8nl

About the Author

This book is the result of a 20-year labor of love, written as a love letter to a state, and out of admiration for an artist. Van Blakely can often be found enjoying two of the main characters of his book: the great outdoors in his native Montana, and classic rock. He makes his home in Missoula with his wife, Molly, daughters Emma and Sally, and is a businessman and railroader.

Printed in Great Britain
by Amazon

25109137R00078